Thomas Votary

Medieval Oxford Coroner

THOMAS VOTARY

MEDIEVAL OXFORD CORONER

ᏀᎻᎬ ᏦᎥᏁᏀ'Ꮪ
ᏀᎾᏞᎠ ᎠᎾᏌᏴᏞᎬ ᏞᎬᎾᏢᎪᏒᎠᏚ

Richard Davies

ᏨᏯ ᏮᎧ

Polar Bear & Company
An imprint of the
Solon Center for Research and Publishing
Solon & Rockland, Maine

 Polar Bear & Company, an imprint of the
Solon Center for Research and Publishing
polarbearandco.org, soloncenter.org

Polar Bear & Company books are available at local bookstores
in many countries, or online, or at info@soloncenter.org.
Retailers may order via Ingram, ISBN: 978-1-959112-01-3.

Copyright © 2022 by Richard Davies
First paperback edition, first printing November 2022
Library of Congress Control Number 2022920876

Cover design by Ramona du Houx includes an adaptation of an illustration
on the calendar page for August from Queen Mary's Psalter (c.1320),
courtesy British Library Board. Double leopard coin images Courtesy
CoinageBritannia, CC BY-SA 4.0 <https://creativecommons.org/licenses/
by-sa/4.0>, via Wikimedia Commons.

Manufactured on durable, acid-free paper in more than one country.

CONTENTS

I

GATES OF AUTUMN, 1345

଼ଃ   ଃ଼

THE ROAD FROM MY FATHER'S manor to Oxford I had traveled a few times in the past, but this day it seemed different, longer, and I viewed familiar sights with a new set of eyes—that of a man in search of his future—wondering if each building I passed might hold the answer. Each traveler on the road a possible employer—from a distance! Every hill I climbed opened a curtain behind which might lie opportunity. Never had I felt more alive!

By midday I had reached the outskirts of the town, noting the increased number of buildings along the roadside, and now and again a sign, roughly painted, indicating a shop or commercial establishment offering goods or a service such as scrivener or tool repair. Oxford was not yet a city, having a population of under three thousand, but it was the largest borough in all of Oxfordshire and served as the market town for all villages and manors within fifteen miles. It was also the home of the University of Oxford which, along with Cambridge, was already one of the leading centers of higher education in England. But my thoughts and eyes were focused on the town and on finding accommodations, both a room and board.

I approached a road running northwest to Woodstock and southeast to London, which crossed my path into Oxford. At the crossroads was the body of one convicted of theft hanging from a gallows. The body or what was left of it, after some time had passed since the hanging, was being slowly eaten by maggots—a reminder that the consequences of crime are harsh. The sight gave me a chill, and the smell of death stayed with me until well after I entered through the Oxford town gate.

* * *

The year is 1345, and I, Thomas Votary, age eighteen, am the second son of Sir Leoric Votary, a knight who served with King Edward III in his campaigns against the Scots. Having little possibility of inheriting my father's estate in Oxfordshire, and nearing the completion of my ten years of schooling at Ravley Abbey, I have sought the counsel of Brother Kenric, overseer of the education of the children sent to the Abbey school, master of the novices, and most importantly, my mentor.

In preparation for deciding what course in life I should follow in the near future and having had some altercation with my father—whether to study to become a priest, return to his manor to learn the skills required to manage it for my elder brother, or to seek a position in the world in which I may use my ability to read, write, think and reason—I opened my heart: "Brother Kenric, I find myself in a quandary. I have learned much here at the school and from you, and I've come to value the application of thought and reasoning, which you have required of me in every task you have assigned. Yet, I question whether these would be tools best used by a priest—or as a layman in the world. I have come to understand that faith and reason are often at odds and often likely to clash, should I follow a religious life. I seek your guidance on how I might serve my faith in a way where it would not so often be in conflict with the tools of reasoning."

After gazing at length through the window, Brother Kenric

turned to me and replied, "Thomas, you ask a most challenging question. One, I fear, that I may be unable to answer to your satisfaction! My own life since the age of seven has been lived within these walls, placed here by a maiden aunt following the sudden death of my father. Since that time, thirty years in the past, I have ventured into the outside world infrequently, and only to study philosophy shortly before becoming a teacher at the abbey, and—" He broke off and looked away again. "And, when I did, it was with great trepidation. Here is my home, my calling—my solace."

Then he spoke directly to me, in a way I shall never forget. "What little I know of a nonreligious life has come from my brief study of philosophy, and my study here at the abbey of the writings of religious scholars—to which I have access in the abbey library. Most of the writers debate with other religious scholars the meanings of faith, truth, honor, duty, justice, and principle—with much attention given to seemingly minor disputes, often over the meaning of a word—and little said about how these values might be applied in one's daily life in the world outside. I have tried to share with you and the other boys who are my pupils what lessons I have taken from these learned men, but I do so only in the context of the life we live within these walls. I have done so in the hope that it would inspire my pupils to choose a life in the Church. I have little to offer you regarding the application of these learnings beyond these walls!—"

* * *

As I walked through the gates of Oxford, the grisly gallows yet upwind, my mind ruminated further on Brother Kenric within the abbey walls.

He had told me it was his belief that there are ways that the values espoused by scholars can be applied in the secular world, outside his walls, but he could cite no real examples. He knows the abbey has benefitted greatly from parishioners who took what they had learned in the abbey school or from the teachings of the parish priests and applied it to their trade and to their family life, becoming generous donors who support the works "we do for the community surrounding the abbey." But he knows not if—or how—they reconcile the conflicts they must face in the outside world.

As I walked, became saddened that my decision between the priesthood and the secular working life may benefit so little from this wonderful man, so long sheltered from the world, the world which I now entered.

His best advice that day was to be always conscious of the potential for conflicts, should I choose to enter the secular world, and to recognize the need always to consider how to live my life in balance—always considering the values and principles I have learned.

As I write, I recall his uncertainty with renewed urgency, his deep personal regret for offering so little help in my decision making. Yet, though he may not have realized it, his counsel throughout my years at the abbey had planted one principle forever in my head: There will always be a right way and a wrong way to act in your life! And the better your choices, the more joyful will be your life. Many a time since passing through those Oxford gates, I have thought about that conversation and how difficult it is to follow that principle. How very difficult.

* * *

I now looked at Oxford differently than I had on any previous visit. The main gate through the wall that surrounded the town put me on the road toward the town center. It was lined with the grand homes of wealthy inhabitants—the moneychangers, major merchants, brokers and traders, accompanied by urban residences for lords whose manors were located in more rural parts of Oxfordshire. In my mind, I compared these homes to my father's manor house and found them ostentatious and not as functional. The homes of merchants were recognizable by their shops at the front, open for display of the goods or services they offered. I was amused by the signs with pictures they posted on their shops, and soon realized that the pictures were intended to inform potential customers who could not read.

The road was filled with packhorses, loaded with grains and other foodstuffs from farms on the outskirts of the town, headed to the marketplace near the town center. The men leading packhorses cried out about the goods they carried, seeking to attract buyers to their market stall, adding to the cacophony filling the roadway. It lifted my spirits with curiosity.

The number of churches situated along this main route astounded me. I counted eight of them between the gate and the marketplace, most with a bell tower rising above the roadway and stone steps leading up to the entrance. The number of religious men, from many religious orders, who moved along the road in pursuit of their duties surprised me. My father's manor supported one priest, and his daily duties were easily carried out in half the day. I couldn't grasp how so many canons, priors, rectors, vicars, chaplains, and friars could be kept so busy every day. Perhaps a town like Oxford harbored many more threats to Christians than did a rural manor like my father's.

As I approached what appeared to be the central marketplace, I caught the smells of a butcher's shop emanating from a street that ran off to the right from the main road. When I walked a short distance down that street, I quickly realized that here was not just one butcher but rather several butchers, each offering a variety of meats, from cattle, pigs, lambs, chickens, ducks, geese, as well as products made from one or another kind of meat—including bacon, sausages, ham, liver, veal, venison, and offal, among others. The area was referred to as "the shambles" by one whom I met on the street. I later learned that this same name is given to such groupings of purveyors of meat and meat products in most larger towns and cities of England. I was overwhelmed by the variety of smells that arose from the butchers' stalls, mixing with those of other butchers and creating an aroma that spoke of both meats—and death. I recalled the smells of death I knew from my father's slaughterhouse, but the smells from the shambles were overwhelming.

At last I made my way to the marketplace and was amazed at the number and variety of offerings made available from the farms within fifteen miles of Oxford. There were several types of beans, carrots, onions, leeks, peas, peasecod, cabbages, garlic, carrots, parsnips, turnips, celery, chibols, colewort, and other items of garden produce too numerous to list. I was, as I say, amazed by this bounty and the variety of pleasant smells that arose here, most from crops I had never eaten or heard of before. This place I would remember and visit regularly, once I found lodging in the town.

As I walked about the marketplace, eying the variety and breathing in the many aromas, I met another young man about my age. I introduced myself and learned that he was a student residing at a boarding hall owned by one of Oxford University's several "colleges," occupied by those enrolled in that college and overseen by a master with whom the students took some of their courses. It was this student's responsibility, this week, to purchase the foodstuffs required to feed the residents. He came with a list of the vegetables, meat, and other items, including a number of coins. He was determining how best to get what was required for the least expenditure of the hall's limited resources. He offered to teach me about negotiating for the best prices, but I asked if he would do so on the morrow, as I had to find lodging before night fell. We agreed to meet later in the week for a lesson. Before I left him, I received his guidance on where I might have the best luck in finding a room. "Stay north of Irishman's Street and Horsemonger Street, the unwritten boundary between the colleges and the area occupied by the townspeople. And tell any landlord or lady you approach that you have nothing to do with the university."

I took his advice, and headed directly towards the northern half of Oxford. It was mid afternoon, and the sun was beginning to sink in the west. I found St. Giles Street, which ran north from Irishman's Street, and followed it in search of signs offering rooms, or people on the street who could tell of places where I might find an available lodging. It took a walk of several sections of this street before I met a man who was able to direct me to the home of a widow who, with her son, rented rooms and, for an additional fee, provided morning and evening meals.

I found her house and inquired on the availability of a room with meals. Her son, Alfred, scrutinized me very closely and questioned me to learn if I was a scholar at the university. I assured him I had nothing at all to do with it, but was seeking work and could pay for the room and meals in advance.

When Alfred was persuaded, he took me to the rear of the first floor to be further checked out by his mother, Margaret Rowley. She probed even further to be sure that I was not an Oxford "scholar," a word she spoke with a sharp look upon her wrinkled face. She asked me to empty my satchel so as to be sure I wasn't concealing any books or implements by which to write. She found no such things, but she did see a small portion of my hoard of silver coins. Her attitude towards me changed most quickly, and a smile passed across her visage for a brief moment. Her next inquiry was in regards to my ability to pay for a room and meals in advance. When I replied in the affirmative, it was as if she had become another person altogether.

I was welcomed to sit in her warm kitchen and join her for a cup of herbal tea. She inquired about my parents, asked from where I had come, and how long I would wish to board with her. My answers, quickly and simply given, seemed to allay any remaining doubts as to my character and ability to pay. I asked her the cost of a room for a month and for two meals per day during the month, and took from my satchel the exact amount she had quoted.

She told me the rules of the house, gave me two keys, one by which I could to gain entrance, and the second to a chest in my room in order to store my valuables. The room was not large, but the bed was adequate, and I had a small glass window which allowed me a partial view of St. Giles Street and a better view of one of the larger churches I had seen on the main road. I felt relieved of my fear that I would fail to find a bed for the night.

* * *

Following the evening meal, I met two others who were also residing at Widow Rowley's, one a tradesman who traveled to nearby villages and manors, offering a variety of small but useful items not readily available in such places. The other, Maurin Barrett, a clerk to Oxford's coroners—often referred to as "crowners"—officers of the crown, more properly called "coroners." The term "crowner" had become widely used in many parts of the realm in place of coroner, based on the Latin phrase describing the office as the "keeper of the crown's pleas."

That evening, Maurin and I decided to walk off the meal with a brief stroll. He told me that in the near future he would be leaving his position as the clerk for Chief Coroner Sir Arthur Houkyn and moving back to his family's manor to become his father's steward. His father was growing old and less able to handle the many duties required. Maurin would learn these and prepare to assume the position of lord of the manor his father wished to give him within a very few years. "It will require plenty of time for me to acquire the skills of my forebears, who were merchants of Venice. As you can see from my complexion, I am not of English origin, nor is my name, unless you forget your Latin, Thomas!"

"Your father must have named you as a reminder." I congratulated him for this advancement in life. In response, he asked if I would like to meet Coroner Houkyn. Maurin knew I was seeking a position in which I could use the skills I'd learned from my years studying at Ravley Abbey and thought I might have what Houkyn required of a clerk. Stunned by his generous offer, I could but stutter my thanks. I had assumed that my search for work would take many days, perhaps some weeks, before being fruitful. And here was an opportunity offered up by a new friend on my first day in Oxford. I could barely contain my excitement and hope. "Yes, Maurin! I would very much like to meet Coroner Houkyn!"

Maurin said he would speak to the coroner on the morrow and ask him if a meeting might be possible in the near future. He noted for me the primary duties of the coroner's clerk. First and most important was to be able to write a good hand and take clear notes that comprise the written record of a case, while the coroner conducted inquests, interviewed witnesses, and interrogated suspected culprits.

Second was that ability to carry on my back or in a satchel the materials—writing materials, including parchment and paper, ink, sand to absorb excess ink from newly written documents.

Third, the ability to prepare and send fair copies of particular cases to courts, when required, and to compile the formal Rolls of cases for the general eyres and other courts.

And, lastly, to remember that as the coroner's clerk one was regarded as a minister of the king and immune from having the writs and other legal documents a clerk carried taken away by anyone, including the sheriff, while being carried by the coroner's clerk.

While we walked on for a while longer before turning back to our lodgings, I can remember nothing of the walk or any conversation we had, as all my thoughts ran towards the great hope of a position of importance to the crown. Surely both my father and older brother would be proud of me at such a young age achieving such an important job! There would be times, later, when I would remember that feeling—and realize how little I knew or suspected of the position.

* * *

The next few days passed quickly as I settled into Oxford, learning its streets and places and waiting to hear whether Coroner Houkyn would deign to meet me regarding the position being vacated by my new friend, Maurin. It was not until the middle of the following week when Maurin informed me that

Coroner Houkyn would see me, on the day after tomorrow, at three hours after "prime" (or "terce," by the tower bells, nine o'clock, as I write since the advent of the new timepieces). Maurin suggested that I write a summary of my education and a list of my pertinent skills. Such a document would demonstrate to the coroner my ability to write a good hand and to summarize the talents I could offer in the position of coroner's clerk. He also advised that I note the name, residence, and circumstances of my father, so Houkyn would see that my lineage came from an Oxfordshire lord with a productive manor owned by a military officer who had served with our king—and an older brother currently serving in the war in France.

I prepared all he suggested, using my best hand to produce a document on parchment which would both record and demonstrate my capabilities. Maurin read it through and acknowledged that I had skills Coroner Houkyn would need. He promised to preview my abilities with the coroner the next day, in advance of my interview. "Maurin," said I, "you have proved a great friend though we have known each other for less than two weeks. I am in your debt and will ever stand ready to repay you in any such way you best need."

"Thomas, it will serve me well with Coroner Houkyn by bringing him my replacement bearing the talents he will need. There may be times in the future when I might need his good will and understanding. It is fair for fair! We both should benefit."

"I take your meaning, but feel I am more greatly benefited by *your* generosity! I thank you very much! Come, let me honor my new friend with an ale at the tavern at the corner of our street!"

* * *

I arose early on the following day and began to prepare for my interview with "Crowner Houkyn" later that morning. I felt my anxiety grow with each passing moment and fought to temper it before my fear of failing overwhelmed me. I forced myself to break my fast and eat the hearty fare set before me by Widow Rowley. The food did help, and I returned to my room to lay out my clothes for inspection. The over-shirt I had intended to wear had a spot on the front, but I had time to clean it with a piece of soap and warm water and allow Widow Rowley to dry away the wetness with a warm iron.

I reread the parchment document I had written yesterday, and was pleased with its substance and clarity. It would be a valuable supplement to the interview I would have with the coroner. At midmorning I left the house in the company of Maurin to walk to my interview. Maurin led me to a small building located down an alleyway off Irishman's Street, where Coroner Houkyn and the other four Oxford coroners had a meeting space.

It turned out to be rather small, as much of what they do takes place around Oxford and in the Northgate hundred immediately north of Oxford, where the writ of the Oxford coroners runs. The workspace was made small by the presence of files of writs, packets of interviews, and evidence gathered during inquests and Coroners' Rolls recording their attendance, and record-keeping of the many courts conducting proceedings within the Oxford town coroners' jurisdiction during the previous forty years.

I had envisioned Coroner Houkyn would be a large man conveying a sense of power and authority. I was but half right. He was short in stature, a bit over five feet tall, but his strong voice reflected the authority of the office of Coroner for Oxford. He greeted his personal clerk warmly and then turned and stared at me, waiting for an introduction. Maurin quickly responded by naming me, Thomas Votary, a new friend, who could take on the duties of clerk that he was soon to surrender. Coroner Houkyn grasped my hand quite firmly and welcomed me. "My clerk has told me of you, but with few details. Please tell me about yourself."

"Sir, my name is Thomas Votary, second son of Leoric Votary, who served with King Edward III in the war against the Scots and was rewarded by the king himself for his courage and for saving the king's life during the battle of Halidon Hill near

Berwick. Our king bestowed upon him a manor in Oxfordshire, south of Oxford, which my father has since developed into a fertile and productive manor. My older brother, Augustus, is now serving King Edward III as an officer in the war in France.

"I have in the past year completed my schooling at Ravley Abbey, just outside Oxford, having spent ten years studying under Brother Kenric, who has taught me to read, write a good hand, and apply reason to the solving of problems. I have written this document to summarize my training and the abilities I have developed in order to go into the world and make a way for myself, God willing. You can see that my writing is clear and legible. I can add and subtract sums. I can read both English and French. Most importantly, I was trained to carry out a variety of tasks with little oversight and to solve any problems I might encounter in the process."

"Thomas, I am impressed with your initiative in writing the document you have presented me. But I must ask, what it is that you know about the work of a coroner? What do you know of the many duties with which we coroners are charged to carry out?"

"Sir, I am not familiar with your many duties, but I am quick to learn, and my understanding is that the duties of being your clerk entail taking notes as you carry out your duties, keeping the notes organized, readable and readily located when you need them, carrying the materials and supplies you will need in order to do your work, and maintaining a list of the court proceedings, inquests, appeals, and other required matters related to the several responsibilities assigned to coroners under law or by order of the king. All this I have learned from Maurin, your clerk, in the last day."

Coroner Houkyn studied my face; I had demonstrated some ability to hear and commit to memory information in a short time. I now kept a respectful silence. Houkyn had a feeling that I could be just the person to be his clerk but needed assurance that I could handle the physical work required. "Thomas, I must visit a manor just north of Oxford, in the Northgate hundred, on the morrow to conduct an inquest over a woman found dead in a hedgerow with no person identified as causing her death. Maurin will be accompanying me, and keeping a record of the information and evidence collected during the inquest. I would like you to come with us. You should understand this important part of the work of a coroner, and you can observe what Maurin does as my clerk. Be here, with Maurin, by an hour after prime, and bring along your horse. The village we must visit requires us to travel a good hour."

I was surprised—and excited—by Coroner Houkyn's invitation. It seemed that he took my interest in the clerk position seriously. And I was most interested in observing the coroner's inquest and Maurin's duties. With a firm voice that belied my excitement, I accepted his request to join them.

Maurin had work to do for Houkyn, so I took my leave and headed back towards the center of Oxford. I had much to consider. I had expected that my efforts to find work in Oxford would take many days and now found myself on the verge of a position.

I set off walking with little attention paid to the direction I had taken and lost track of time before I stopped to see where I was. I found myself in a small square. The men around me were all young, and they wore garments which told me they were scholars at one or another of the colleges. I had been warned to stay clear of that part of the town, because there was a history of fighting between scholars and Oxford residents in places like this, where both groups considered it their territory. But those fights tended to occur in the evening—when the growing darkness provided cover and allowed fighters to disappear quickly and avoid identification by the beadles who patrolled the streets on behalf of the town's officials.

I looked enough like a scholar and attracted little notice as I walked. I was feeling hunger and sought about for a tavern or food shop. Before too long, I entered a street with both food shops and a tavern. I chose the latter. My eyes, so use to the bright autumnal sun, took a few moments to adjust to the darker interior. It was well attended, mostly men in work clothes enjoying an ale and a hot meal. I found a half-full table and took a seat. A serving girl approached without delay to tell me what dishes were available this day and to take my order for a bowl of lamb stew and a small tankard of ale. She quickly returned with my ale and promised that the stew would soon come. I had taken only a sip before she placed a generous bowl in front of me. As she had no unserved patrons, she took a moment to sit at the table and rest her feet. "I've not seen you here before. Are you new in this part of Oxford?"

Yes, I told her, having come to town but a week ago. "I came seeking work, and earlier today I met with Oxford's chief coroner regarding a possible position as his clerk. He asked me about what skills I would bring to the job, and I think my answers were well received. I am to go with him on the morrow when he conducts an inquest in a village a few miles north of Oxford. His invitation makes me feel that he considers me worthy of the position."

She, who is named Rebecca, congratulated me on my good fortune. "He thinks you may indeed serve him well!" We talked a few moments more until two men entered the tavern, and she left me to greet them.

I relished the lamb stew, and the ale was nearly as good as that brewed on my father's manor. I made short order of both and looked about for Rebecca. I wished to thank her and to say I would return to the tavern. She was busy but saw me wave to her as I prepared to depart. She managed to come towards the door before I left and wished me well. I knew then for sure that I wanted to know Rebecca better.

Back on the street, I used the sun's position to orient my route to Widow Rowley's boardinghouse and managed to see parts of Oxford I had not visited previously. It may not be deemed a city, but it is large in its various neighborhoods. It would take me some time to become familiar with its many parts.

II

DEATH UP-CLOSE

⊂B ⊃

THE DAY DAWNED TO CLOUDS and a cool wind, but before I broke my fast the sun showed on the church tower down the street from Widow Rowley's boardinghouse. I quickly ate a bowl of sweetened porridge with bits of apple and slipped another apple into my bag for later. Then I donned my second-best shirt and britches, slipped my feet into my boots, threw my cloak around my shoulders, and both Maurin and I headed to the stable to retrieve our horses, mine rented for the day. It would be a short ride to meet Coroner Houkyn, then a longer ride to the site of the inquest the coroner was to hold beginning at midday in the Northgate hundred village of Islip.

"You are wise to dress warmly for our journey," Maurin commented, "as we are at the will of the wind for near an hour in each direction. I have been to Islip village twice while in Houkyn's service, and each time experienced changes in the weather while on the road. Better to be overdressed than under!"

I asked Maurin, "What can you tell about Islip, and the purpose for the inquest?

"There was a body—of a young woman found hidden behind a hedgerow." The cause of her death is unknown, as is the person or persons involved. The inquest is the coroner's opportunity to view the body, collect information from the first-finder of her body, and any other information about the woman, the location of the body, whether she was moved after her death, and the likely cause of her death—if there was any physical evidence found, such as a weapon or scrap of clothing not belonging to the woman, which might help identify the person who committed this heinous act. The coroner will ask questions of anyone who might have information to add."

"It sounds much like a puzzle, scrambled up and needing the pieces rearranged to make sense."

"Aye, that is a fair description of the challenges facing a coroner. Some puzzles are easily solved, but others defy solution!"

We were approaching the place where we would meet Houkyn, and I could see him ahead. Maurin had brought along the materials needed to take down what was asked and answered at the inquest, as well as any questions and comments at the site—paper, several pens, ink, sand, a portable desk for a hard, smooth surface. Houkyn met us and added the Coroner's Roll and several sheets of paper bearing notes he had made in preparation. It was obvious that he took his work seriously and sought to instill a similar attitude in his clerk.

I believe that Maurin had adopted Houkyn's attitude but had grown tired of the pain, suffering and death so closely associated with the coroner's duties. It came to me that the opportunity to become the steward on his father's manor allowed him a way to leave without acknowledging how mentally painful being Houkyn's clerk had become. My thought came, not from anything Maurin had said, but from the look on his face as he loaded Houkyn's notes to the bag of supplies he would need at the inquest—and how he looked to me as his way out.

It took but a few moments of preparation before we mounted and set off north on the road into the Northgate hundred and then a less-traveled road directly to the village of Islip. Leaving the walled portion of Oxford through the northern gate, the

Northgate Road was well traveled and maintained, built to handle the heavy use of farmers, traders, the steady stream of commerce moving north and south. The road was wide enough that farm wagons could pass one another going in opposite directions without need for either to pull aside.

I noted the numbers of wagons, oxen teams, horse carts, and other wheeled vehicles coming south. It was autumn, and much of this southbound traffic was bringing the products of the recent harvests to the largest and most diverse marketplace in all Oxfordshire. The nearly four thousand people living in Oxford and the several thousand who live in nearby villages relied on this southbound agricultural trade, as well as the inflow from south of Oxford, to furnish a great variety—the aforementioned beans, carrots, cabbages, onions, parsnips, peas, peascods, squashes, garlic, apples, cherries, a variety of berries, figs, dates, grapes, pears, plums and quinces, and many herbs, to extend my list somewhat. And the farmers certainly relied on the coins they took in at the markets to purchase supplies available locally and only in Oxford, as well as cloth, pottery, foreign herbs, medicines, wine, and seeds for new varieties of fruits and vegetables they would plant in the spring.

We turned off the main road and took the less-traveled westward-heading road for Islip and the site of the inquest. The surface became more uneven, and we needed to slow our pace to allow our horses to negotiate the ruts. While Islip was about two miles from where we turned off the main road, it took us the better part of an hour thereafter.

Fortunately, we had allowed extra time to reach Islip and for Maurin, with my assistance, to lay out the Coroner's Roll, writing instruments and related items. Houkyn was ready to proceed with the inquest in a timely fashion. But the sheriff's deputy, who had been notified of the day and time of the inquest, had not arrived with the jury of twelve local men he was required to empanel. Houkyn was clearly angry that neither deputy nor jury was present, but he told us that gathering twelve men for a coroner's jury was sometimes a challenge. And he and his fellow coroners from Oxford made it a practice for the coroner convening the inquest to inspect the body without the jury present. This was based on the belief that the coroner's skill and experience resulted in a more complete and detailed examination than a jury of twelve local men could produce. The jurors were allowed to conduct their own examination once they arrived at the inquest, and in some few instances they observed details missed by the coroner.

Houkyn, Maurin and I accompanying him, began his examination of the dead woman. By law, the body was required to be naked, so that the coroner could more easily discover evidence of the cause of the death. Houkyn proceeded in a very organized fashion, beginning at the head and moving slowly along the torso in search of anything that might enable him to determine the cause of death. When he reached her feet, the body was turned over, and he began working his way back to her head. As he worked, he occasionally would have Maurin make a note of something he saw—a scratch, bruise, or puncture of some sort that might be related to the death. It was not until he had the body turned over to expose her back that he found a penetrating wound located on the left side of her back, in the area of her ribs. It was a narrow slit between two ribs, which he almost missed, because there was no sign of blood. He spotted it because the skin adjacent to the slit was slightly puckered.

He turned to Maurin and had him note the wound and remind him, when the deputy and jury finally arrived, to inquire of the "first-finder" whether the deceased was found lying on her back. If so, he wanted to examine the place where she was found in hope of evidence of blood on the ground. Because the weather during the past two days had been dry, blood should be found at that site. Houkyn turned to Maurin and me and whispered that if no blood was found, it would mean that she was likely killed elsewhere.

Houkyn then completed his examination of the body, discovering no other signs of foul play. What he did find in the hair on the back of her head were pieces of dried birch leaves.

He had Maurin make note of the leaves, particularly the type of tree from which they came. He wanted to see what types of trees were located close to where she was found. If there were no birches in the vicinity, it would strengthen the argument that she had been killed elsewhere and moved to where she was found. His examination complete and no sign yet of sheriff or jury, Houkyn suggested we pause and have the food he had packed for our trip. He got no objection from either of us, and in short order all was washed down with ale.

During the meal, the coroner turned his keen attention to me and asked, "Thomas, you have now observed the examination of a dead body—probably for the first time. Did it cause you distress to see death up-close? What did you think of the process of examining the body for evidence of the cause of her death?"

I heaved a sigh and replied, "It was the first time I have been so close to a dead body, but I was so drawn into your examination that I didn't think about it being dead. Your question caused me to feel sad about her death, but I did not feel repulsed by its presence."

"That is a good sign, Thomas! If you are to become my clerk, you must be able to separate the deaths we investigate from the work you must do as part of the investigation. If you become caught up in the emotions brought on by death, you will find it too difficult to do your job properly."

"Sir, I believe I can separate the death from the investigation."

Just then we heard the sounds of several people arriving at the inquest site. It proved to be the undersheriff and the twelve locals he had impounded as the coroner's jury. The undersheriff did not apologize for this late arrival but explained that he had had to pound on many doors in the village of Islip in order to get the required number of jurors. He then identified the twelve men by name and status in the village, in order to satisfy Houkyn that these jurors were reputable and trustworthy members of the community, free from any known conflicts that might color their judgment.

Houkyn had each juror answer under oath. First, he asked

the juror if he thought the death was caused intentionally, by misadventure, or naturally. Second, if done intentionally, was it suicide or homicide?

Then he proceeded to ask the jurors, as a group, a series of questions intended to discover the circumstances of the death, any details they knew about the death, which they might know because they lived in proximity to the deceased.

First, he asked jurors if they knew the deceased. Was she a local resident or a visitor to Islip? Was she known to associate with any resident, male or female? Was she married, single, or widowed? What was her reputation in the community? Had she been seen recently in the company of a person or persons known or not known in the community? Had she ever been involved with a man of the community not related to her? Had an unknown man been seen recently in or near Islip?

Some of the jurors reported that the woman was a local resident named Alice Johnson, age twenty-three and unmarried, who had recently been seen talking with a man named John from the nearby village of Brackley, where he lived with his aged mother. John was believed to be about twenty-six or twenty-seven years of age and also unmarried. There had been no reports of any trouble between the two.

Another juror reported that he had seen a man of unknown age, but probably younger than forty years, pass through Islip during daylight hours, on three occasions in recent weeks. He had not been observed speaking with any resident of Islip and might live in the village of Ettington about three miles northeast of Islip. No other juror reported seeing anyone in the company of the deceased, nor any person unknown to the village passing through Islip in recent weeks.

The coroner directed the undersheriff to send a man to Brackley for John and another man to Ettington to inquire about the man who would have passed through Islip. Both of the sheriff's men were to bring in each person or learn their whereabouts. Houkyn also released the body of the deceased girl to her family and authorized them to bury their daughter.

With the inquest finished for the day, to be resumed if and when one or both of the men were brought in by the sheriff's officers, Houkyn recessed the proceeding and sent the jurors home with an order that if they became aware of any additional information about potential culprits they were to notify him as soon as possible.

Maurin packed up his writing supplies and the Coroner's Roll containing his notes from the inquest, and we secured them away in his saddlebag. Meantime, Houkyn went out and walked about the village to stretch his legs and to see again the place where the dead girl was presumably found, as the identity of the first-finder remained uncertain. He walked among some birches and looked about for evidence of blood but found none. He hoped the sheriff's deputies had recorded any other evidence that might help in finding the killer. But that information would have to come at a later date, much to his displeasure. Now it was time to return to Oxford.

We mounted our horses, and Houkyn led us back towards the main road running south. Along the way he asked Maurin if anything he had heard during the inquest had struck him as odd or unusual. Maurin replied that there was one member of the jury who seemed very uncomfortable with the proceedings, particularly when Houkyn asked jurors if there was anyone else they would like to have come before the inquest. That juror's head had been moving back and forth repeatedly as if he feared that another juror might mention his name.

"Which juror was it?"

Maurin recalled his name was Hunter. He was of middling height, had a beard and reddish hair that was parted in the middle. Beyond that, he couldn't add anything about the man or his behavior. Houkyn said he would inform the undersheriff and ask him to make inquiries.

The rest of our trip back to Oxford was without incident, though near the end the winds picked up out of the northwest and chilled us. Winter was not far off, and there would be occasional bursts of snow in the next few weeks. We arrived at the coroner's meeting place, as dusk settled over Oxford. Maurin and I bid Houkyn a good evening and rode back to the stables, handed off our steeds, then walked back to Widow Rowley's, arriving just in time for the evening meal. It had seemed a long day, and I retired to my bed as soon as the meal was through, fell asleep forthwith. My last thought before sleep was about the juror who had acted suspiciously. He had been shaking his head back and forth as if to discourage other jurors from naming him. That stuck with both Maurin and me and in later months would come back to me.

III

NOBLES AND GROATS

ଔ ଓ

T HE DAY FOLLOWING THE ISLIP inquest dawned clear and cold, and I felt it even beneath the covers on my bed. I considered rolling over and returning to sleep but quickly recalled the request Houkyn had made to me as I prepared to depart the coroners' meeting room the previous evening. He had asked that I return this morning so he could discuss the position soon to be vacated by Maurin. That recollection changed my plan for more sleep and quickly made me begin to put on my clothes in preparation to comply. The thought of working as Houkyn's clerk excited me more than I had anticipated. I was proud of the fact that I had come to Oxford only ten days ago, found a place where I would have meals and a bed, and was about to have a position as clerk to the Oxford coroner, a crown officer. In my wildest dreams I never thought I would be at this point so quickly.

Finished dressing, I went to the kitchen to break my fast and tell Widow Rowley that I expected to have a job by the time I next saw her. She was genuinely pleased with my seeming good fortune and wished me luck in my meeting with Houkyn. Fortified against the cold by a bowl of porridge, I put on my winter cape and stocking cap and strode out the door.

The wind could be heard whistling around the church tower at the corner of the street, but I felt it very little because the buildings were set so close together that the gusts were unable to reach ground level. But I felt it when I reached the first cross street and needed to pull my cape closer for warmth.

Sped along by the desire to be at the coroner's meeting room before Houkyn, I quickened my steps and lengthened my stride until I was nearly running. I soon neared the meeting room but was surprised to find Houkyn already there, looking over Maurin's notes from yesterday's inquest.

"Thomas, I am pleased to see you this early in the day. The work of the town's coroners knows few bounds of time. We may be called out to view a body before the sun rises or well into the evening, and my clerk must needs be with me whenever and where I must go." He then invited me to sit across from him at his work table, so we could talk about the position he must fill posthaste.

"Thomas, you have now observed an inquest, the kind of investigative work in which a coroner is often engaged. It is a critical part of our most important function—determining the cause of a death and whether it was murder, misadventure or natural causes. There are other duties we also carry out, the most frequent being to appear in the courts of Oxford and of Oxfordshire to provide those courts information pertinent to cases before them. The conduct of inquests is the beginning of the legal process. Without these investigations into unattended deaths, the legal system would flounder. My question to you is this: Are you prepared to perform the duties required of a coroner's clerk? The position brings little honor, but without your close attention and accurate recording of what is said at an inquest, we cannot provide the courts with the information which would be the basis of their decisions. What say you?"

"Sir, I am prepared to work for you. I understand the importance of the work that coroners do and that the records

I produce based on the questions and answers spoken at an inquest are critical to the courts. If you make me your clerk, I will work hard to carry out my duties with diligence and skill."

"Thomas Votary, based on the commitment you have just made, I appoint you as our clerk. You have many of the skills and talents required of the clerk, and have shown the ability and commitment to learn the other talents you will need to do your work as clerk. I welcome you!"

"Thank you sir! I accept your appointment!"

Following this formal discussion and Houkyn's appointment of me as his clerk, our conversation became more relaxed. He told me about my compensation, which was initially set at three shillings and four pennies each week, plus six pennies for the cost of boarding of my horse in the local stable used by the five coroners for their own horses. He told me that I would be required to dress appropriately as his clerk. As I am the son of a knight, the sumptuary laws allow some freedom in my attire, but Houkyn required that I dress for my job in a way that is neither ostentatious not flamboyant. He recommended clothes which are in muted colors, such as brown, black, grey or white, so as to cause me to be unnoticed during inquests and court proceedings. As my attire was currently what I wore while in school at Ravley Abbey, I would need to find a tailor in Oxford who will make clothing in line with Houkyn's recommendation. I would also need to purchase a sturdy but inconspicuous steed.

Houkyn also told me that I should be at the coroners' meeting room on the days when the coroners would also be working there. He noted that there are days when the coroners would take care of personal matters related to their manors, commercial endeavors, or family issues. He informed me that they were elected to positions as coroners by the town's knights and freeholders, and they are paid no salary for their work. As clerk, I was to be paid from the pockets of Houkyn and the other four coroners.

On the first point, it was evident to me that the absence of compensation was galling to Houkyn. He was a knight and a freeholder who raised grains and beans on his land and sold what he raised in the Oxford farmers market. His profit from those sales, after subtracting his costs, were modest. And the parcels of his land which he leased to smaller farmers generated just enough income to allow him to serve as coroner. He was not a wealthy man. No wonder he felt put upon.

I was reluctant to ask why coroners were not compensated for the important work they are asked to do, and he offered nothing on the issue. No wonder there was frequent turnover in the ranks of the five coroners.

On the way back to Widow Rowley's, my mind was spinning about my appointment as the clerk for Houkyn—and its many implications. I was now employed and needed two sets of new clothes. I had not yet met the other four Oxford coroners and hoped they would be as receptive to me. As Houkyn's clerk, I would serve all five coroners. Could I do all the work the five required? Would the other coroners resent the wages, taken from their pockets, that I would be paid? Could I learn the complicated relationships between the different Oxfordshire courts where the coroners were often required to attend and provide information collected on the Rolls, some of which were pertinent to the courts even though the Coroners' Rolls are from ten or fifteen years ago. That long delay between the event in question and the consideration by the Court of General Eyre was due to that court circulating slowly around England, often taking seven years or longer to complete its circuit.

I had worked myself up worrying about all the possible problems and challenges I faced as the new clerk, but as I walked I realized that Maurin and the clerk he had replaced both had managed to learn about the several courts and had a working relationship with each of the coroners. That realization brought a gradual calming for me, and by the time I reached the Widow's, I was feeling much better about a challenge that would be dire indeed to fail, among the relationships of family and community.

Based on the advice of Chief Coroner Houkyn, I was not

going to talk about cases being handled by the coroner's office. He had told me of some examples of information, gathered by the office early in an inquiry, which had been conveyed to one or more outsiders—information that had been repeated to others including, in one instance, to a person the coroners thought might be the one who had committed an as yet unsolved murder. In that example, the suspect suddenly disappeared and was reported to have left Oxford. Houkyn wanted to make sure that I understood the possible consequences of allowing confidential information gathered in a coroner's investigation to reach others beyond the coroners. He made it clear that such an action would result in dismissal, at minimum. Based on that advice, I made a decision to avoid any discussion of any investigation with any person.

As I arrived at the Widow Rowley's, the evening meal was being brought to the table. During the dinner conversation, I told the widow, her son, and the other residents that I had just been hired as a clerk to the Oxford coroners, taking the place of Maurin, and left the matter at that. The widow congratulated me on my new position and others around the table echoed her. Her son asked what the coroner's office did, and I briefly responded in general terms, saying nothing about any specific matter. The diners moved on to other topics, and I breathed a sigh of relief. Thankfully, questions about my new position did not come up again that evening.

I asked my fellow diners for information on where I might find a tailor who could make me a set of clothes suitable to my new position. Only the Widow Rowley's son had experience in getting work clothes made. He told me there was a tailor he had used several years ago, who had a small shop a short distance from their house. He offered to take me there and introduce me.

"Thank you, Alfred! I would be pleased to have you introduce me to this tailor. Is there a day and time when you would be able to make that introduction?"

"Thomas, I could take you to meet him tomorrow morning

following the breaking of our fast. Would that be good for you?"

"Yes, that would be a good time for me also."

Thus, on the morrow, Alfred and I left the boardinghouse shortly after the second hour after prime, heading north and then east, until he stopped at the entrance to Clothiers Alley. As was true for such professions as butchers, this alley was where anyone seeking some type of clothing would go. Alfred led me down the alley near halfway and stopped in front of a modest building. At the front was the tailor's business location, a single, long room running across the entire front of the building. When we entered, it was clear that there were two additional rooms, set behind the front room, where the tailor had two apprentices cutting cloth or pinning together parts of garments in preparation for being stitched together.

The tailor, named Roberto, was from Florence, but his speech was nearly without accent, suggesting that Roberto had been living in England for many years. Alfred waited until Roberto finished giving direction to one apprentice regarding a garment, and then introduced Roberto to me, saying that I was beginning a new position and needed new clothing that would meet the specifications of my employer.

"Thank you, Alfred, for bringing Thomas to see me! I am surely able to make the items required." Turning to me, he added with emphasis, "Thomas, tell me what you require, and I will make it for you."

I related to Roberto the specifics given me by Houkyn, including the colors of fabric, in order that my presence would attract little or no attention from witnesses being questioned at inquests. When I completed the summary of my needs, I asked how quickly he might be able to tailor them. Roberto thought for a moment. "One week!" He then had me stand straight and still, so he could take the measurements. Then he directed me to a room further back in his building, where he kept bolts of fabric. There he recommended quality, weight and color for each item. I agreed with all his suggestions but one. He had suggested a bright white linen for the shirts, but I told him I needed something not so bright. He tried to change my thinking but recognized that I was not to be persuaded. "I understand," he finally acquiesced.

We resolved all but the price. He considered the fabrics, the time to cut, fit and stitch up the garments, and added his profit. He quoted the price of one pound, four shillings, threepence. It was acceptable, and I paid him half on the spot. He told me to call again a week from this day, at the bells of terce. We shook hands, and Alfred and I left.

"Alfred, your assistance in this matter has been invaluable! May I buy you an ale and a bowl of stew as thanks for your aid?" I took him to the tavern I had first visited. My hope was that Rebecca might be there. On entering, I caught sight of her busily serving beverages and hot food to a pair of men, one of whom I had seen at the central marketplace on the day I had arrived in Oxford. Rebecca quickly recognized me and came our way when she'd finished with the pair. "Thomas, I will come by to serve you once I've brought ales to three patrons in the rear."

I thanked her, then refocused on my companion. "Alfred, you and your mother have been so helpful to me as I have sought to find my place in Oxford and to adapt to the requirements of my new position. I am in your debt!"

We talked about the work I would be doing as clerk, but I carefully turned the conversation away from the particulars of the inquest. I asked him whether he had always lived in Oxford.

"No, Thomas, I was born on a manor located east of Oxford town, where my father was the steward, and my mother was the manor's brewer, in charge of making ale and other alcoholic beverages for the family of the lord and for the families who worked the manor lands. She was very skilled at brewing and had a reputation, both on and off the manor, for the variety and quality of the beverages she made. Unfortunately, the manor owner was been convicted of failing to pay certain taxes on alcoholic beverages, and mother had to give up her duties as brewer. The new lord was so disappointed at losing her as maker of ale that he agreed to pay her to teach some of the women on the manor the arts of brewing. He also promised her a substantial sum should one of her students become as skillful as was she."

"Was she successful in that endeavor?"

"Aye, she was! One of the women followed my mother's lessons very carefully, and in a few months was able to make the his lordship's favorite ale in a way that satisfied him and pleased my mother greatly."

"Did his lordship live up to his promise?"

"Yes he did. And he presented to her a purse filled with golden coins. These she kept in a secret place, known only to her and my father, to support them when my father could no longer do the work as steward of the estate. Unfortunately, that time came sooner than expected—and in a most horrible way. While helping the plowman who was attempting to calm one of the oxen in the midst of a thunderstorm, the ox stumbled and fell against my father, crushing both of Father's legs. So broken was he that neither his lordship's own physician, nor a renowned doctor in Oxford was able to save him. He lingered several days, but in the end the damage to his body was too great, and he died."

"What a terrible accident! I am so sorry for your loss!—and your mother's. When did this occur?"

"It was but four years past. The new lord was saddened by the death of his steward, who had served him well, and he sought to make life better for my mother. He offered to assist her to find a new source of income, so that she could support herself—and me."

Just then Rebecca returned. I ordered two of the tavern's best ales and asked what might be available for a hot meal. She told us they had a hearty chicken stew with vegetables or leg of mutton on a trencher served with carrots and leeks. I asked Alfred his pleasure and joined him in ordering the chicken stew. Rebecca came back quickly with our ales and promised that the stew would arrive before we finished them. She was good to her word and placed large bowls before us in short order.

Once we had taken the edge off our hunger with steaming spoonfuls of the stew, I pursued the story about Alfred's mother, following his father's terrible death. "How did you and your mother come to be in Oxford?"

"It became clear that there was no future for my mother on the manor, and it was likely that she would need my help wherever she would spend the rest of her life. We talked about what might provide sufficient income to allow her a decent life and enable her to have neighbors with whom she might enjoy the company and conversation. For these she needed to be in a town or large village. His lordship had given her the gift of a leather bag which contained many coins, including silver groats, half groats, English pennies, farthings, and a few of the new gold nobles and half nobles. Including the coins she had received from for teaching a new brewer, all the coins added up to a substantial sum, sufficient to get us situated in a town where she might purchase a boardinghouse.

"Oxford seemed promising, and I spent time seeking a house with sufficient rooms to produce enough income to provide what was needed. I quickly learned that serving scholars attending Oxford University was risky. The relations between the Oxford scholars and the residents of the town were often contentious, with battles between the two groups occurring too often to justify a house in the student quarter. I searched in the areas occupied exclusively by longtime residents with no connections to the university. Within a few days, I found the house now owned by my mother. The owner had done well in a local business and wanted to move where his success would be reflected in a more prominent dwelling. I offered him a sum for the house, and with a bit of haggling we struck an agreeable price for the property and some of the furnishings—which he deemed not worthy of the house he was about to acquire. That was five years ago, and we have had the good fortune that comes with growth in Oxford's resident population. Seldom any period when we lacked a full house. I have no doubt that we will have a boarder to take Maurin's place as soon as he leaves."

Alfred and I were preparing to leave the tavern, and I waved to Rebecca, intending to pay for our food and ale. She saw my wave. I gave her several coins and thanked her.

IV

QUESTIONS OF BEHAVIOR

℘   ℘

THE NEXT DAY, I RECEIVED a message from Coroner Houkyn that I was to report to the coroners' meeting room to begin work on the following Monday. My first duty would be to begin familiarizing myself with the Oxford Coroner's Rolls. Information required for the conduct of court proceedings regarding offenses and allegations were "enrolled" on parchment and kept in files categorized by court and date. I was both excited and anxious about my first day as the clerk. The need for an accurate record of all of the proceedings held by the courts was a daunting task. I will need to devote all my attention to recording in words the essence of what is said and to identify objects referenced during an inquest or other proceeding.

Maurin told me that he had similar thoughts when he became the coroners' clerk three years before but learned how to do the required tasks in short order. He believed I could do the same. I was about to find out.

When I arrived at the meeting room, Sir Arthur Houkyn was there, as were Oxford's other coroners. Sir Arthur introduced me to Lord Morcant de Whatele, Sir Ricard Eynsham, Lord Ricard de Adynton, and Sir Torsten de Geddyng.

He informed them that I was the new clerk, that I had recently completed my schooling at Ravley Abbey and had demonstrated to him my ability to write a good and clear hand, to take notes at inquests, and to carry out the various duties required. He said that I was the second son of Sir Leoric Votary, the lord of a manor south of Oxford and trusted knight who fought beside the king in the war against the Scots and played a heroic role in the battle of Halidon Hill. He also noted that my older brother, Augustus, was an officer in the king's army now fighting in France.

I was well received and was offered their aid should I need help understanding the various duties for which I would be responsible. Houkyn shared with his fellow coroners the document I had written about myself. "It persuaded me," he intoned, "before I asked him a single question, that Thomas had the needed skills to perform the work of clerk. I think you will come to a similar conclusion once you see how he does recording the information in our next inquest."

Houkyn then turned their attention to the need to prepare for the next meeting of the county court. "We can expect the court to have a large number of cases to hear, as the approach of the winter urges them to address as many as possible. The difficulty in gathering, during the winter, the many people whose testimony is required to complete the court's work on any case makes the November session a busy one, as we well know!"

The coroners then reviewed the cases expected to be on the docket in November, with each coroner identifying those cases on which they could be called to provide the information from the Coroners' Rolls—with the aid of their new clerk.

Normally, the clerk finds in the Coroners' Rolls the notes on each case to be considered by the royal justices, but they would assist me this time in finding the needed records. By the time of the January county court session, with the help of the coroners, I should be ready with the Rolls.

Houkyn released the other coroners and had me join him in a review of the supplies I would need at the November county court meeting. He had the list which Maurin had previously prepared. We were short of ink and parchment paper, so Houkyn wrote out the amount we would need and gave it to me, along with sufficient coins to enable me to purchase these items from a local print shop with which the coroners did regular business. He told me where the printer was located, and sent me off to make the purchases. Before I left, he gave me a key to the meeting room, so I could store them when I returned.

Houkyn said that he had personal business to transact, and would not return to the room until the day after tomorrow. He advised me to look through a recent Coroners' Roll and study how Maurin had recorded information from a recent session of the county court. "It will help you prepare for the November session," he warned.

After Houkyn departed, I soon recognized the pattern of the court's proceedings. As each case was called up by the justices, Maurin would begin a new record. He would note the name of the proceeding, usually named after the person, or persons, involved in the case. The persons named were those whose behavior had led to arrest by the sheriff. Next Maurin listed the offense which these named people were accused of having committed. What followed were notes regarding the evidence presented by the sheriff, the evidence, if any, offered by named parties, the substance of any testimony made by the sheriff or one of his deputies, and testimony from the accused. Next, Maurin made note of any judgments issued by the justices, any penalties imposed, usually financial in nature, and any appeals those "in the dock" might make to a higher court for reconsideration of the evidence or the judgment. Lastly, he listed the specific Coroners' Rolls needed should a question be posed to the coroner who handled that matter.

Seeing how Maurin recorded the information from an inquest, I began to feel more confident that I would be able to capture the records the coroners would need to document matters that courts would need in order to carry out the provision of justice. I thought about the fact that some of the courts of the realm were required to travel the length and breadth of England, hearing cases and making judgments based on the written words clerks like me had written as much as seven years previous. Could such a process, so long removed from the acts and events in question, result in justice?

Unable to answer my question, concerned as I was about my own fate, I returned in haste to the Rolls to make notes about the particular language used during court proceedings. I wanted to recognize the specific phrases a judge used frequently, so I could memorize them, in order to write them out quickly and not miss the substance of what followed from their lips. It seemed to me that I, the clerk, would have an important, perhaps outsize role in assuring that the information from an inquest would be clear and understandable for a judge, who would have it recited by some future coroner years after I wrote it.

After several hours of reading what Maurin had written, I replaced the records and wondered if inquests were the only duty required of coroners. I made a mental note to ask one of the coroners. Then I returned to the Widow Rowley's for the hot meal, about which I had been really thinking during the last hour. And I speculated on how my work would compare with that of my brother in France. Was it a just war? A question I would keep to myself, for the nonce.

* * *

The county court convened three days later, with all the coroners and yours truly in attendance. I would have the duty of recording any decisions or directives issued by the judges. But the coroners had a greater responsibility—that of answering questions from the judges. Those answers should be found in the Coroners' Rolls recorded by Maurin and occasionally by an earlier clerk. If the answer required more specific information than that coroner could recite from memory, I was to have the Coroners' Roll containing the details of that case ready to hand. As I was new, one of the other coroners would have that

Roll opened to that case and would hand it to me to be put in front of his colleague being questioned. At future county court sessions, I would need to be prepared to have the Roll open to the correct case—and in time to be able to mark the point where the coroner would find the section of our records where the answer was to be found. It all seemed overwhelming.

The county court met for two full days hearing the details of the eleven cases on the docket. At the end of each day, the judges retired to deliberate. While they might reach a judgment, I was told by Houkyn that they wouldn't announce the decisions until the day following the completion of their hearings and then would announce each decision in the order in which the case had been considered. Thus, on that third day the county court judges reconvened at midday. All parties in each of the cases were present and speculating among themselves, when the chief judge stood to begin the announcements.

The coroners gave little thought to the fairness of decisions rendered that day, being more interested in what effect their work on each case had had on the judgment rendered. Upon the closing of the county court's session, the coroners and I retired to a nearby inn to discuss the role our office had played in each case—and if there might have been something we should have done, but didn't, that had affected the judgment. Over a meal and pitchers of the inn's best ale, the discussion flowed from case to case, generally lighthearted and seasoned by assessments on who had made the best presentation—or the biggest mistake. It was the first time I felt part of the group, and I liked the sense of comradeship, which gave one the feeling that justice had been done.

When we broke up, Houkyn had me join him in walking back to the coroners' meeting room, where we would put the Rolls back in storage and leave notes along with my writing supplies. He told me that I was learning very quickly how to do the job and would soon be ready to learn more about the other duties required of coroners. He said that many of the duties placed on early coroners had subsequently been eliminated—like "appeals and outlawries"—or had been assigned to others, like "treasure troves and wrecks at sea." But "abjurations of the realm" and special duties regarding financial matters were still under the coroners, though the latter was often done in conjunction with the sheriff. As we parted at the meeting room, I asked Houkyn if he would sometime tell me more about those little-needed duties and those no longer part of the work of coroners. He agreed to do so someday soon and waved me on with that benevolent smile of one who sees excess in the eagerness of inexperience.

* * *

As I walked back towards the Widow Rowley's, feeling a mixture of excitement and loneliness, I thought about Rebecca at the tavern. It would be some time before dinner, so I changed course for the Hawk and Hare. Entering quickly in hopes of finding her there and not busy, I asked the man behind the bar. He was unsure, not having seen her for a short while, but the bar was not busy, and he agreed to check in the kitchen. In a trice, he was back to say she had left but would return tomorrow to work at prime. I asked if I could leave a message and whether she could read. He wasn't sure if she could but promised to tell her my message.

"Please say that Thomas Votary, a young man who met her twice at the tavern, asks to see her again. He will come to the tavern on the morrow when business is less busy, in hopes that we might speak." I pressed a penny into his hand and promised another if he has delivered my message and she has told him she will speak to me. He thanked me and promised to tell her immediately upon seeing her the next day.

I walked away from the Hawk and Hare with hope—and excitement. I knew some of the peasant girls whose families lived on my father's manor and had sometimes played games with them, like hoops, stick ball, and stilts. But I had never before been close with one girl and now was having feelings towards Rebecca that I had never experienced. I said a prayer asking that she be pleased with my message and agree to walk with me soon. Then I wondered if a prayer to have the physical pleasure of being with a girl was somehow sacrilege. Brother Kenric had given me no knowledge of the nuances between sex and love. What a mix of conflicting feelings!

That evening I sought to reason with myself concerning Rebecca and a possible "relationship" with her. I thought back to my conversations with Brother Kenric. He cared very much for the welfare of the boys who studied with him, and they often sought his good counsel. Like them, I often asked advice regarding my interactions with the other students as well as my studies. Looking back on the ways I dealt with the disagreements, squabbles and little traumas that seemed daily occurrences, I wished that the school also had females as students. Perhaps I would have been better prepared for developing a relationship in the outside world and not so confused about my feelings at this moment. But it was not to be, and I had to figure it out on my own.

I was up the next morning before the dawn, unable to wait for my return visit to the Hawk and Hare. I broke fast with a roll and some butter, then bathed and quickly dressed. Alfred, also up early, had a quizzical look when he saw me. "Where are you headed so early this morning? It's too early for your clerking duties!"

"I am feeling quite energetic this morning and thought to take a brisk walk through Oxford in order to be more familiar with the town. It's now my home, and I should know my way around it." I hoped he wouldn't press for more.

"Good for you Thomas! I wish I had such motivation on such a chill and damp morn. Though I have lived here for more years than you, I must admit to knowing only the parts of Oxford, where my work or family duties take me. I look forward to hearing where you go and what you see."

While he had been speaking, it dawned on me that the Hawk and Hare would not be open for business for at least an hour.

I could walk about a good part of the town as yet unknown to me. Setting out, I decided it was time I become more familiar with the area dominated by Oxford University. During daylight hours, the area would be busy with scholars going to and from lectures, causing little trouble for the residents living adjacent to the district.

But a short walk south of Margaret Rowley's boardinghouse, I soon reached it. At this early hour, the others I met were not scholars, rather the men and women who served them—porters, washerwomen, cooks, all on their way to work for the day. The number of these workers was surprising. I had no idea that Oxford University's several colleges represented such a large part of the population and its livelihood. There were older women, backs already bent as if they were cleaning the streets they walked; young, strapping men, fit to lift and carry things of some size or weight; and younger men and women, some younger than my own eighteen years, likely going to prepare food for the scholars and teachers, who seemed to reside together in large houses. This surge of workers heading to the university each morn and departing each eve, seemed to go unnoticed by most Oxford residents, who awoke later and were home earlier and eating their evening meal. I wondered where all these laborers lived.

The flow of traffic ebbed quickly once the town's tallest church tolled its matins bell, calling the faithful—unencumbered by early work. It seemed that the bell served to separate in two Oxford's many classes of residents, leaving each half almost unaware of the lives and work of the others.

I kept walking! By my reckoning, the Hawk and Hare would open shortly to serve members of the business community needing a place to meet and discuss their transactions while breaking their fast. Rebecca should be there preparing to serve their meals. With that thought, I reversed course and headed towards the tavern in hope of catching her before she was too busy to talk with me.

The tavern lights were lit, but the public entrance was not

yet open. I skirted around the side of the building and made for what proved to be the kitchen. Poking my head into the room, I asked the first person I saw if Rebecca was about. He replied that she had just carried clean mugs to the barkeep and should return shortly. I waited but a few moments before she returned to the kitchen and she was told I was there. She quickly came my way.

As she didn't know me beyond my first name, I reintroduced myself and spoke quickly about our previous meeting on a busy day in the tavern. She seemed to recall it, but I knew that she must have dozens of such contacts each day, with most recollections fading away almost before they could register. Then I said I had left a message for her with the barkeep the previous evening, asking if she might be willing to take a walk with me—at her convenience. This registered with her, and she smiled. "Thomas, I thank you for the message you left for me! My work fills much of my day, but I don't have to work on Sunday. Could we walk that day?"

"So surprised by this sudden, wonderful question, I was too tongue-tied to respond immediately but regained my speech. "Yes, Sunday! I can walk that day."

"Good! What time of day should we walk?"

"How about in the afternoon—when it will likely be warmer than in the morning?"

"And where should we meet to begin this walk," said she, with a bit of a smirk on her otherwise smiling face.

Catching the tease in her voice, I smiled back and said, "Let us meet here on Sunday afternoon at the bells of sext. I'll await your arrival in front of the Hawk and Hare!"

"I must return to my work now, lest I get in trouble with the owner. I will see you on Sunday noon, as planned." She leaned forward, placed a light kiss on my forehead and was gone.

It was more than a few strides out of doors before I was able to take in what had just occurred. I could hardly believe my good fortune. Rebecca had said yes! I walked, but I did

not know where. All I could think about was Rebecca. At
last I came to my senses and realized that I now was south
of Oxford University and nearing the south gate of the town,
though how I reached this point without passing familiar
landmarks, I couldn't say. I was far from the Widow Rowley's
street and must have approached this place from the eastern
part of Oxford. My only recollection of what I had passed
was a mansion set back on a large lot amid many old trees and
protected by a tall fence.

There was nothing scheduled that day at the coroners'
meeting room, but I needed to clear my head and put my Sunday
walk with Rebecca in perspective. I set off towards the meeting
room intending to review what I had written during the recent
county court sessions. The sun was warming, and by the time
I arrived I would not need to start a fire. But to my surprise, I
found Coroner Ricard de Adynton also there, in the company
of a man I had not seen previously.

Not wishing to overhear, I went to the other end of the long
chamber and took out my notes. While reading, I caught some
of what Coroner Adynton was saying, even though he spoke in
a low voice. It seemed the conversation entailed money—quite
a bit, apparently—and who was to receive some or all of it. I
must admit the conversation gained my attention, so I tilted
my head to hear better, while maintaining a posture of one
deeply focused on my own notes. They spoke for just a few
moments more; then de Adynton stood and escorted the other
to the door, then stepped outside with him. They talked another
moment, and the other man left.

Coroner de Adynton returned to the room, put a piece of
paper from the table in his pouch, and made his way to my
end of the room. He greeted me and inquired why I was here.
I explained that I wanted to do my work properly and was
reviewing my notes from the county court proceeding from the
previous week.

He told me that he occasionally used the meeting room as
a convenient place to meet those with whom his manor did

business. "I sometimes sell grains or sheep that are in excess of our needs in order to obtain silver and gold coins needed to acquire additional land. This man buys grain from me."

I did not wish to appear too interested in his conversation and said only that I hoped my work did not disturb him today. He appeared satisfied that I had not overheard anything and soon took his leave.

I wondered whether there was more to his conversation than a grain sale. I was sure I had heard talk of "a large amount of money." Did he have such a prosperous manor that he could make a sale able to bring him a large sum of gold and silver? Perhaps he did.

I finished my review of notes and made some corrections to them before leaving. I was beginning to feel part of the coroners' work, learning the subtle details. It felt good.

Heading back to the Widow's house, I went by way of the central market to see what fruits and vegetables might be available, to bring something for her kitchen larder. There were fewer sellers than I had seen when I had arrived only seven weeks before, but they continued to have a good variety on offer. I purchased a half bushel of hard apples, which should last a couple of months before going by, and a large lump of ginger—to enliven a variety of dishes. I was feeling a part of Margaret Rowley's expanded household, and a part of Oxford itself. A nice feeling.

When I reached the Widow's, there was a package waiting for me—the garments! Also there was a letter, brought by a courier sent by my father, in response to one from me two weeks previous, by way of a man visiting Oxford on business, whose tavern was but a mile from the manor house. Father asked if I might be able to visit him before winter set in and had enclosed some silver coins, "to keep you from want!" I laughed at the thought but was appreciative of his interest in how my life was progressing, in spite of his skepticism.

He also told me that he had received a letter from Augustus, with King Edward in France. It had been sent some five months earlier but had not arrived until just a week ago. He was well, and the king's army was driving the French army backwards. As it was early summer when he wrote it, Father presumed that the English would be building a winter encampment in a strategic location and sending out raiding parties to seek supplies of food being stored by the farmers nearby. They would offer to buy the food, but if the offer was foolishly rejected, they would take it as a spoil of war. Armies always travel by their stomachs, lawful or not.

I prayed my brother would be safe and well, return home soon, victorious. On the morrow, I would ask Houkyn if there would be a time before the spring, when I might be able to travel to see my father for two days and then return.

While I was reading the letter and thinking of my family, the Widow came home to find the half bushel of hearty apples and the lump of ginger I had placed on her work table. She was touched by the gifts and began peeling some apples to be baked with a bit of cinnamon and a tiny bit of the ginger. We would enjoy the treat this evening with dinner.

The fragrance of the baking apples permeated the air around the dinner table, and all of us were anxious to finish our meal so as to get to the baked apples. When served, we wasted not a moment in plunging our forks into this sweet, tart dish, and the cook was rewarded with many comments on her masterpiece. She glowed with pleasure over all the kind words.

A short time after, I excused myself from table and retired to my room. I had much to think about—something good, like the anticipation of my walk with Rebecca, and something questionable, like what I had overheard from Coroner de Adynton and his unknown companion at the meeting room.

I took the pleasurable matter first and considered what I might ask her while we walked. How did she come to be a young girl living and working in Oxford? Does she live with her family? Where had she lived before Oxford? What are her duties at the tavern? Was she treated well by the tavern owner? What does she do when not working? And each question seemed to prompt another. If only I can make these questions not seem like an interrogation, but rather a conversation with her questions of me interspersed with mine. At last, satisfied that I could have a conversation with her, I turned to the meaning of what I had overheard from de Adynton.

The talk of a large amount of money seemed a subject not in keeping with the work of the coroners. Could this be something more than just inappropriate words spoken in an inappropriate location? Was de Adynton engaging in some sort of scheme that went contrary to the oath he took when elected an Oxford coroner? I tried to think about the words said while putting them in the most favorable light. He is the lord of his manor and has every right to buy and sell the crops and livestock he raises. But it was hard for me to understand what he could sell that was worth "a large amount of money." And what was meant by that phrase?

To me it would be a handful of gold florins or the new double leopards King Edward III was supposedly having minted in gold this year. But what would it mean to an owner and lord of a manor? Ten times a handful? A hundred times? Even more?

Then I thought about whether this was a conversation I should mention to Houkyn. Perhaps he already knew about what de Adynton was discussing. I didn't want to seem ungrateful for my job as clerk, or worse, a tale-teller! But what if this was a bribe they were discussing in return for the other man to avoid paying a large amercement penalty?

The more I thought about this, the less inclined I was to blurt it out to Houkyn. Instead, I decided it was more prudent to engage Houkyn in a general discussion of the many forms of amercement that were levied regularly by the judges on people who failed to do what is required by law or judicial edict. I had seen the county court judges amerce several parties and witnesses. Perhaps this might lead into a discussion on the ways those amerced tried to avoid the prescribed penalty. In such a way, I might prompt Houkyn to speak about what de Adynton might be doing. This felt like a safer way to broach the subject of bribes without suggesting that any coroner was doing something illegal or unethical. My mind was at ease about this approach, and I was able to fall asleep shortly and soundly until the dawning of the morrow.

* * *

The weather was cold when I emerged from the boarding-house, so I went back to get my cape. I also decided to get my horse from the livery stable and give her some exercise as I rode to the meeting room. It had been almost a week since I had ridden, and she was happy to get out into the brisk air. Bayardine and I were still getting to know each other, since I had purchased her recently at the stables. I took a roundabout route, so she could stretch her legs and walk off all the grain she had eaten since our last ride. And when we reached the meeting room, I gave her a carrot. She chewed it up fast and nuzzled my arm to see if there was more where it came from. I tied her to the post in front, next to a horse that I recognized as the one Houkyn had ridden to the inquest in Islip some weeks ago.

When I entered, Houkyn was talking with a sheriff's deputy about a body discovered in the University quarter, for which the cause had not yet been determined. Houkyn was directing the deputy to notify residents and college masters in the area that an inquest would be held tomorrow at midday into the death of an unnamed male found in close proximity to their residences. It was to be held at the town hall, and any resident or college master who was notified but failed to appear was at risk of amercements. The deputy departed quickly to go door-to-door in the area where the body had been found, notifying the people who were to be the coroner's jury at the inquest.

Turning to me, Houkyn gave some details of the death and instructed me to join him and at least one other coroner here at the room at prime the next morning to prepare for the inquest and take the necessary supplies. It was not the right time to broach the issue I had considered. It would have to wait a few days.

From what Houkyn had heard from the deputy, it was a young man perhaps under twenty years of age, who was found face down with a wound in his back. It looked like it had been made by a blade. There were also signs of a struggle, though how many were involved was not clear.

While he was describing what the deputy had told him, Houkyn decided it would be helpful to visit the body where it yet lay, to see what more could be determined and if there was any evidence that hadn't been reported by the deputy. He asked me to join him, saying I had good eyes and asked good questions. I was surprised at this compliment and quickly agreed.

We headed off to view the body in the place where it was found, and while we walked Houkyn told me the sorts of information he would be looking to collect at the scene. The first thing to seek was the weapon, probably a knife. He said that it was common for the killer to toss aside the weapon near where the fight had occurred. We should search the bushes, wooded areas and high grasses as the best places to dispose of even one's best knife. No sense for the killer to hold on to a good knife if doing so would incriminate him.

Once we completed a search for the weapon, the next step would be to look for a shoe or boot print in soft dirt or mud. If we found one or more, we should measure its length, width, and the depth to which the print had gone into the ground. We should also note any distinctive markings left on or by the footwear, like a deep cut in the sole or the outside of the print being deeper or shallower than the instep. This could tell us that the culprit might have a deformed leg or foot or a pronounced limp.

Lastly, Houkyn said we should look for evidence indicating the direction from which the culprit had come to the scene or had left it. Knowing either or both, the coming and leaving direction could point where to search next. By the time he finished his guidance on evidence, we had come upon the scene.

Having uncovered it, we stood back a few steps from the body; it had already been denuded by law. Houkyn surveyed the location. Pointing towards an area of longer grasses, he directed me to start at the far end and carefully examine the edges of the grassy patch for any signs that someone had recently walked into or through the area. Then I was to look very closely for signs of anything, not just a knife, having been dropped or thrown into the high grasses, disturbing the spot where it fell. If I saw any such evidence, I should stand still and point towards the bent grass or other sign of disturbance until he could observe for himself. Meanwhile he would inspect the corpse.

I did as directed, and very slowly moved from right to left along the front edge of the tall grass. About a third of the way along, I could see where something had distorted the natural flow of the blades of grass about three feet in from the front edge. I called to Houkyn. He broke off from his examination and came to where I stood pointing out the disturbed area. It was too far from the edge to reach the spot without disturbing the grass further, so he carefully pushed apart the grasses along a straight line from where he stood, only stepping forward after being sure there was nothing of note along that line. Then, kneeling either side of the disturbed area, he pushed the blades apart and looked closely at the exposed ground. He saw nothing at first, but as his eyes adjusted to the shadows, he reached forward and picked up a small leather pouch, damp from the dew. He stepped back and out of the area in question.

He deftly untied a knot that held tight the closed pouch. Pulling it open, he lifted something out. The look on his face was astonishment. He held ten gold coins, apparently double leopards, the new coins just now being produced by King Edward III's mints.

"From where could these new coins have come? The king has not allowed these to be released!" He jingled the gold gently in his palm. The coroner's puzzlement over the brilliantly colored coins was soon replaced by speculation. "The king has several royal mints spread about England, but only one is within fifty miles of Oxford, and that is the Reading Royal Mint, established by the Abbot of Reading several years ago.

"There are two questions we need answered. First of all, how were these coins removed from the Reading mint, the most likely place of origin? Second, why did one of the two people involved in what appears to be a murder throw aside the pouch in which we found the coins?"

I boldly responded by suggesting a third question. "Did the one who tossed away the pouch do so to hide the coins or to protect them from being taken from his possession? The answer to this question will likely shed light on the answer to your second question and possibly on the first."

Houkyn acknowledged that my question put the pouch and its recovery in a different light. Was the deceased a royal messenger delivering the new coins as directed by the Abbot of Reading? If so, to whom? Could it be a thief who had found a way into the abbot's counting room while spying on the minting of these coins?—and seized the moment to grab a pouchful before their formal release?

"Sir, you and I may be the only people who know this trove of gold coins has somehow made its way to Oxford. Should we travel to Reading to inquire about these coins which have traveled here, and to determine if they came as intended, or illegally?"

"Thomas, yours is a good idea, though I first want to have a private conversation with Sheriff John de Alvetone and see if he was informed that any of these coins were coming to Oxford. If he was not made aware of their arrival, we will ride to Reading and meet with the abbot."

We then returned to the search for anything more that might answer questions about the murder or help identify either the victim or his killer. But another hour spent turned up little—just a piece of fine, grey fabric, which appeared to have been ripped from a coat, but not the victim's.

We returned to the coroners' meeting room to place the piece of fabric in storage and lock the ten coins in our strongbox. We retrieved our horses from the tie-out post and parted, I going back to stable my horse and then walk the street leading to the Widow's. Where Houkyn traveled to, I did not know.

The sun was well on its way towards setting, and the air began to cool. November in Oxfordshire could be nearly as warm as October, but if the winds shifted to come out of the north, it was more like December. This late afternoon was beginning to feel a bit like the latter.

I was excited about what we had found at the murder scene, but knew better than to mention it or even the murder, which would soon be common knowledge. To avoid saying something I shouldn't, I sought to steer the conversation during the evening meal to the weather, the letter I had received from my father, and the prospects for the king's army in France (and the role being played by my brother, Augustus). We all commiserated over the coming winter winds and hoped that the snows would arrive in small doses, never so deep as to paralyze the town. There were stories of memorable blizzards past and tales of people stranded in their homes for several days before the winds or the neighbors removed enough snow to free them.

The war in France produced much speculation on both English and French fortunes and on what might prove the turning point towards an English victory in what seemed an endless war. My fellow diners were very interested in Augustus's role in the fighting. I knew only a little about it but built up every bit of information until some began to believe he was leading a large company of archers and swordsmen into battle. Little did I know that the fantasy I conjured for those around the table was fairly close to the truth.

When I told them that I hoped to soon travel to my father's manor for a brief visit, they were quite excited for me. Several there had not seen family for more than two years, and hoped that they too might be reunited soon with their loved ones. I was asked about my father and how he became the lord, where his manor was located, and what were the crops there. The conversation expanded, and others talked about how towns like Oxford were dependent on the food and fiber raised on the manors and small farms in more rural areas within traveling distance of the town. I pointed out that the manors and farms also produce people, and some produce more people than are needed to do the work of growing and harvesting crops and livestock. I pointed to myself as an example. Others nodded in agreement. More than half of those at the table had left villages or manors for Oxford, because they were not needed or wished to find work or a career that was only available in larger towns and cities.

V

REBECCA'S STORY

☙ ❧

FOLLOWING OUR MEAL, ALFRED AND I stepped outside for some fresh air. There was a breeze out of the northwest with the promise of frost by morning. If the winds continued from the northwest, we could expect either a cold rain or the season's first snowfall. I voiced my hope that any snow or rain would hold off until after Sunday afternoon. Alfred looked at me quizzically then asked what was so important about Sunday afternoon. I told him of Rebecca, and the walk we were to take the next day.

"Where did you meet this girl?"

I reported on my three visits to the tavern. "I don't know her well but feel something when I'm with her—excitement—in a way I have never known before now, and I want to understand why. Do you understand how I am feeling? Can you tell me why I feel this way?"

Alfred told me that he, too, had had feelings about a girl when he was younger. "I didn't understand it then any better than you are now, but I've learned since that what I felt was lust. A powerful urge to have my way with her physically! And I didn't know what to do or how. I didn't know what I should do—or how to do it, only that I wanted to be with her forever. Later, I heard from a priest that my feelings were sinful and that I needed to stay away from any girl who made me feel that way. But I couldn't accept the priest's admonition and sought out ways to ease my feelings, if only momentarily."

I suspected I knew what Alfred did to stop those feelings and was afraid to ask him; he seemed too embarrassed to pursue the subject. I would go for my walk with Rebecca without any reliable advice on matters of sin, love and lust—except the wise choice not to avoid all women to whom I may be attracted.

I awoke early on Sunday, after a restless night during which I thought about what I might say to Rebecca during our walk. Awake now, I could recall only a few topics which had entered my head during the previous night, including "Where she had come from before Oxford," "Did she enjoy her work at the Hawk and Hare," and "What she did when not working." I was hopeful that each of these would lead to a broader conversation.

The morning passed very slowly, and I became more anxious about the "Walk with Rebecca." I even considered the idea of not meeting her at all! But as the time approached, I grew calmer and began to prepare to leave for the Hawk and Hare. In the open air between the boardinghouse and the tavern, the anxiety faded, and I quickened my pace. When I arrived she was not there, and I feared that she had decided otherwise. But she rounded the corner a moment later, and strode to the tavern to meet me.

I greeted her warmly and thanked her for being willing to accompany me for a walk about town. She returned my greeting and asked in which direction we should stroll. When I wet my finger and held it up into the wind, she looked quizzical and asked why I was checking the wind.

"Because walking into the wind would make conversation difficult."

"How thoughtful! I appreciate your consideration. Based on what your finger has told you, in which direction should we go?" she asked—with just a hint of jest in her voice.

"I believe we will best enjoy our walk if we go where the

houses and other buildings block the breezes, rather than draw them. Doing so will also keep us from the bitter cold." She then took my arm and we headed down the nearest street that fit with my proposal. It was but a matter of moments before we were shielded and busy talking.

"Rebecca, how long have you lived in Oxford?"

"I came here ten months ago, arriving during a snowstorm with nothing but the cape around me and a pouch in which I had five silver pennies and my mother's shoes. I was cold, hungry and very afraid."

"Why were you traveling in such weather?"

"I was seeking a better life than what my mother had. She had died but three days before, and I knew my fate if I stayed."

"What was the fate you were facing?"

"I would become the ward of the lord of the manor on which we lived, a man whose reputation among his peasants was very bad. He was cruel, and he claimed the right to test the virginity of every peasant girl when she reached fifteen years of age—just an excuse to ravish them all. I was approaching that age when my mother took ill and wasted away. She died on the day before I turned fifteen, and I knew he would claim his right over me on the day following her burial.

"I searched our home for warm clothes and for the few coins I knew she kept in hiding. Our friends on the manor gave me two silver pennies, a sharp knife, and the wool cape I'm wearing today, and they told me how I could gain my freedom. I left immediately after her burial, and never looked back!—"

"My God! what a terrible situation you were in. I'm so glad you were successful in making your escape. How many days did you travel before you reached Oxford?"

"I was on the road for eight days. I would find shelter each evening, sometimes with a family I met and other times in a wooded area where I could cut some boughs from fir trees to make my bed and to cover myself while I slept. I looked for apples still on a tree, or even scrumps on the ground, and twice I found abandoned shacks where I could sleep. Being a young girl on the road, there were risks, but also people who felt sorry for me and shared their meal and home for a night and sent me off the next day with an oatcake or bread with butter. I finally reached the outskirts of Oxford on the eighth day and passed through the town gate in the company of a farmer carrying produce to the farmers market. He vouched for me as his granddaughter at the gate, and I was allowed to enter. I found shelter that night in a church."

"Your story shows you to be very courageous. Once you made it safely to Oxford, how did you manage to keep body and soul together?"

"The priest at the church, he allowed me to remain there for two nights while I sought work. On the manor I escaped, I had betimes worked in the lord's kitchen and was a server when he gave a banquet. I began seeking positions as a kitchen slavey or a server. I was hired at the Hawk and Hare. I started as a kitchen helper and quickly learned how to do almost every job in the kitchen but that of cook. The owner liked my hard work and how quickly I learned each job. One day, when one of the servers in the tavern didn't show up, he had me put on a fancy server's apron and go to work in the tavern. By the end of the first day, I felt at home as a server. Before long, I had learned how to chat up customers and how to handle those whose consumption of ale or spirits led to misbehavior."

"I observed your skillful handling of your customers on the first day I came to the Hawk and Hare and the seeming pleasure you took in the exchanges with patrons. Felicitations on your well-won freedom!"

"Alas! I am away from the lord, but under the law I'm not yet free. To gain my freedom from the lord of the manor, I needed to reach a town or city and live there for a year and a day. Only then would I legally be free from his ownership and control.

"If I remain in Oxford for another two months and a few days, I will have lived here the required time. I am counting the days—and frequently looking over my shoulder to see if anyone is hunting me."

"Rebecca! I will do all in my power to see that you complete the year and a day to secure your freedom. One who has faced such adversity deserves as much justice. You can count on my support and if needed my protection. I will not let your former lord steal your freedom from you!"

"I am most grateful for your offer—and your support!"

We walked on, neither speaking for some distance before she placed her hand in mine. I had a peaceful feeling and pressed her hand against my cheek. I had never before known this sensation and hoped it would never end. I put my arm around her shoulder and drew her closer to me.

We walked on, arms around each other, neither wanting to end the feeling of being together, but the sun subsided towards the horizon and shadows lengthened. Very soon it would be too dark. I steered our walk in the direction of the Hawk and Hare, thinking that Rebecca and I would go our separate ways. But as we approached the tavern, she told me I could walk her home, rather than to the tavern. Overjoyed, I quickly agreed. She said that she lived with two other women and a brother of one of them, in a small house only a few blocks from the tavern and gave me directions.

We quickened our pace, now in the wind, still with our arms about each other, already at ease in step, and soon reached the house. We pressed lips lightly in promising kisses and said our goodbyes, until the following Sunday. I turned towards the street that led to the Widow's.

VI

LOVE AND EVIDENCE

ᘓ ᘔ

NEARING HOME, I DECIDED TO say very little about my walk
with Rebecca. It was too soon to speak about our budding
relationship, and I would never speak about the secret she had
shared with me, until the time had passed, and his lordship
could no longer drag her back to the manor—legally—and
likely subject her to unthinkable treatment. Fortunately, when I
entered the house, I found that I had missed the evening meal,
so I would not have to face the questions of my fellow residents.

Rowley had saved me a large plate of servings of most of
the elements of dinner, all but the dessert of baked apples
with cream. The food was cold, but I enjoyed every bite,
regretting only the absence of the apple. I thanked her for her
thoughtfulness and went discretely to my room.

The following morn, I rose later than usual and found that
my fellow residents had all left for work. I hoped that when we
were together for the evening meal again, the table discussion
would not include my time with Rebecca.

I broke my fast with some of the Widow's biscuits and a
bowl of oatmeal sweetened with a bit of honey. Then I headed
to the coroners' meeting room, hoping that Houkyn would

be there, so we could talk about a possible trip to the king's
Reading mint and, hopefully, the conversation I had overhead
between de Adynton and the unnamed man regarding "large
amounts of money."

At the livery stable, I mounted and rode to the meeting
room. I was glad to see Houkyn's horse tied up outside. But
when I entered, I saw that de Adynton was also there, along
with Coroner de Whatele. Houkyn was telling the others about
the murder near the university district and our finding of the
pouch filled with the double leopards. He called me over to join
them, and told how his method for examining a murder scene
had led to the stunning discovery.

De Adynton was most interested in the coins, and both
coroners questioned how these newly minted coins, not yet
released by the king, had come to be in Oxford and possessed
by one involved in a murder—either culprit or victim. Houkyn
had no immediate answer but told them that he and I would
soon travel to Reading to make inquiries with the officials at
the king's mint, located near the Abbot of Reading's church
annex.

The other coroners were taken aback by his decision to have
me travel with him to Reading, but he made it clear that I had
played a key role in finding the place where the pouch had been
tossed and that I deserved the opportunity to join him as he
investigated this aspect of the murder.

The conversation turned to the inquest and the directive
that Houkyn had made to the deputy to round up residents
living near the site. He asked Coroner de Whatele to conduct
the inquest and told us that he had spoken with Oxfordshire
sheriff John de Alvetone, and they had agreed that the inquest
should be held on the following Monday, the day when Houkyn
and I would be traveling to Reading.

Coroner de Whatele was pleased to have the leadership of
the inquest and immediately began preparing himself to direct
the questioning and any cross-examination he felt warranted.

Houkyn had left the meeting room to find a courier who

would ride to Reading before the morning was over, carrying an official request to meet, on Monday next, with the master of the king's Reading mint and such others as may have knowledge or information pertinent to our investigation. As a result, de Whatele asked me to give him a detailed description of the murder scene and the body, a listing of such evidence we had found at the scene or on the person of the dead man, and Houkyn's thoughts (as told to me) regarding what had happened. Feeling as if I had suddenly been elevated in my position, I offered to provide the information he requested on the following day, promising to give him my best recollection of the investigation and our conversation trying to piece together the events leading up to the murder.

I found de Whatele already at the meeting room the next morning. We sat together at one of the tables, and I proceeded to give him my report.

"Thomas, that was a very clear and detailed recollection! I am impressed with your mastery of the details and your ability to present the evidence in a way that allows me to manage the inquest as if I had been part of the investigation from the start. Where did you learn the skills you just demonstrated?"

"Sir, I recently completed ten years of schooling at Ravley Abbey," I reminded him, "just outside Oxford. My teacher, Brother Kenric, spent a good portion of his lessons during my final two years there teaching me how to think and reason logically. I learned that truth is best determined through the collection of information that rests on facts and is interpreted by applying reason and logic. While such a process in not foolproof, it is more likely to produce a correct interpretation than any other method of thinking. A good beginning is more likely to lead to a correct result."

"You have certainly demonstrated an ability to analyze information in a way that leads to better understanding of the evidence and of the behavior of people involved in a murder. You are a good addition to the Oxford coroners' group!"

I thanked him for his very kind words and said that I looked forward to working with him when the opportunity presented itself. "If you have further questions on this murder before Houkyn and I leave for Reading, please send a messenger to the house where I am currently boarding, and I will come to you at the meeting room as quickly as possible."

Soon afterwards, I returned to the boardinghouse to consider what I would need for our trip to the mint. I understood from Houkyn that Reading was about twenty-two miles from Oxford. By my estimate, we would spend at least seven hours in riding there, with another hour or two that we would need to rest our horses and take nourishment at a tavern along the way, plus of course a similar amount of time on the return trip. Our visit to the mint and the questioning of those concerned would likely occupy one or two days. So I planned to have sufficient clothes with me for twice as many days, away, and sufficient coins to pay my expenses.

Then I turned my thoughts to Rebecca and our next walk, which was to be on the Sunday before my Monday trip. It being late morning, I decided to walk to the Hawk and Hare for an ale—

I reached the tavern with brisk abandon and entered. Not wanting to create a problem for Rebecca, I was careful not to occupy too much of her time. When she came to take my order, I only requested the ale and asked that she think where we should walk on Sunday and give me her thoughts when she returned. She moved on to take an order from another patron and soon arrived with the ale. She whispered that we should go to the winter farmers market, where she would purchase some vegetables for her dinner. Thinking that was the extent of it, I asked where else we could go. She whispered in my ear, "To my house to celebrate."

Not understanding what she wished to celebrate but happy for an opportunity to be together away from the cold wind, I agreed to meet her in front of the tavern.

I sipped my ale slowly and used the time between sips tactfully and rather helplessly to watch Rebecca as she worked her way about the tavern. She had a graceful way about her as she took orders and brought her patrons their food and beverage, often exchanging pleasantries or asking how they were doing this day. In the rare instance that a customer took issue with the food or drink, she had a way of resolving it in a pleasant, accommodating fashion, offering to bring another drink or have the cook fix the problem.

When she next came to my table, I told her that I was to accompany Coroner Houkyn on a trip to Reading, beginning on the day after our Sunday walk, and that I expected we would be gone four days, returning in the evening. She wished me a safe journey and good luck in our mission, and then she slipped a handkerchief from her apron pocket and gave it to me—to remember her by whilst I was away. I smiled and thanked her for it, upon which she spun on her heel and headed for another table, where a customer had just seated himself.

My ale finished, unable to think of food, and with work to be done before the Monday departure, I headed for the coroners' meeting room. I wanted to prepare a detailed description of the dead man. I also wanted to summarize the pieces of evidence we had found at the scene, hoping one or more might trigger a thought from the chief of the king's mint in Reading or any of his underlings. It took me the first half of the afternoon to put together these two documents until I was satisfied. I carefully folded the two sheets of paper, slipped them into my pack, and left for the Rowley house again.

Along the way, I stopped at the farmers market in hopes of finding something special for the Widow's larder. This late in the season, the items still available were fewer than even a week previous, but I was in luck. One stall had pears, still hard and free from bruising, due to good storage. The price was a bit high, but I purchased six good-size ones. As the afternoon was but half gone, there was an excellent chance that the Widow might be able to turn some of them into a tasty conclusion to the evening meal. Motivated, I hurried the rest of the way and arrived just as she was beginning her preparation of dinner. She was pleased and quickly decided to make a pear cobbler and to use the remaining piece of ginger.

"As you will be away from Monday morning until Thursday evening, I have ordered a large roast of pork for our Saturday dinner, knowing there will be sufficient left over that I will pack up for you, along with half a loaf of bread, to carry on your trip and eat along the way."

"You are wonderfully thoughtful, madam, and we will savor every bite of it!"

* * *

Four days passed quickly. Saturday dinner was delicious, as anticipated. The roast pork succulent and well-seasoned, with carrots and turnips aplenty, and two bottles of red wine that Alfred had purchased earlier in the week. The food and wine fed the conversation around the table, with each of us sharing stories and memories of our younger days. The pear cobbler, flavored with honey and ginger, prompted memories of meals each had been fortunate to enjoy, and we closed out the meal on a very pleasurable note. My fellow diners wished me well on my journey to Reading and tried in several ways to learn my reasons, but I would say only that it was in connection to my job as clerk to the Oxford coroners and that I was accompanying the chief coroner on the trip. There was a mix of envy and trepidation on my behalf and demands that I give them details when I return. Through all this I remained sufficiently closemouthed, the wine notwithstanding.

Afterwards, I stepped outside for a few breaths of the cold, winter air. Then I retired to my room to contemplate my walk with Rebecca and, as she had whispered, "to celebrate," on the morrow. I thought how nice it would be to have time with her and those with whom she shared the house, but the "celebration" was a mystery. I blew out the candle next to my bed and fell asleep, wondering what she had meant.

I awoke later than usual on Sunday, rising well after the sun, and took a bath in the wooden tub set in an alcove off the kitchen. Alfred had partially filled it with water from the kitchen hand-pump, before he had gone to bed on Saturday night, allowing the water to warm a bit. This morning the Widow had asked him to carry two kettles of water heated over the stove. Once bathed, I quickly toweled off and returned to my room, so the next tenant could take his bath. I returned to the kitchen forthwith, fully dressed, and ate a bowl of hot oatmeal with a bit of milk poured over it.

By the time I had finished it was midday, and I was due to meet Rebecca on the steps of the tavern to take our second walk in about an hour. Quickly I brushed my hair away from my face, chewed on some licorice bark to clean my teeth and breath, put on my boots and heavy coat, and headed out. The wind was blowing from the north with sharp ice crystals stinging my face. I quickened my pace to reach Rebecca and arrived just as she turned the corner of the street which passed in front of the tavern.

Her cloak was nearly threadbare, and the snow had melted in places where the fabric was so very thin. Her face was flushed by the icy wind and the rapid pace at which she was moving, in spite of the load she was carrying. She ran into my arms and hugged me hard, seeking warmth and protection from the elements. In my embrace, the flecks of snow and ice began to melt and run down her face. Feeling in my pocket, I pulled out the handkerchief she had given me the day before and mopped up the droplets until her face was dry.

"Before I started for the tavern, I went to market," she said. "I was sheltered from the wind, and no snow was falling. But when I turned the first corner, I walked straight into the wind and felt the ice. I tried to stay on streets where the buildings shielded me from the worst, but I had to walk into the wind when I turned the next corner. I feared I would freeze before I reached you. But, thank God, there you were ahead of me on the steps!"

I took the load of vegetables. "I think walking today is

unwise. Shall we return to your house and get out of the cold and snow?"

"Yes, please! Can you hold me up while we walk back to my house? I don't think I can make it on my own."

I wrapped my arm around Rebecca's shoulder and took her hand to steady her as we struggled to get away from the open space around the tavern. We needed to get onto the adjacent road, where the buildings would provide a partial windbreak. Traveling no more than the hundred feet seemed to take forever, but we finally turned onto the road and immediately felt significantly less wind, but even then it came between the houses, and for a few moments we were required to endure its force and chill.

Fortunately, the road we were on took us through a wooded part of Oxford, and the trees formed a much better shelter than the intermittent houses. Rebecca was able to stand still a moment and realized that we were nearly to the road where she lived. This gave her a burst of energy, and we arrived, exhausted, bone cold, but safe again.

Opening the door, I lifted her across the threshold, slammed the door and threw the bolt. I helped her towards a chair in the kitchen, placed the market goods on the table and turned to fetch a few sticks of wood. I tossed them onto the meager fire burning there. The dry wood caught quickly and burst into flame, and we felt the increased warmth against our frozen faces and hands. Only then did she sink onto the chair with a deep sigh of relief.

Hearing the racket we were creating, one of the young women with whom she shared this house came out of her bedroom to learn what was going on. Seeing Rebecca in such a state of exhaustion, she rushed to her aid, but the warmth of the fire was already bringing us around. "I'll put some water on to boil and make tea for you both," she offered, and placed a filled pot over the flames.

Thereby we were sipping a sturdy herb tea. Rebecca sometimes shivered uncontrollably, but the tea and the fire eventually brought back the color to her face. She took my hand and kissed it.

"You went to market without me!" I chided lovingly.

"It was too cold for romance," she replied with a smile.

It became clear to her housemate that we were both nearly fully recovered, and she retired to her room, leaving us alone together. We sat with my arm about her shoulder, and her hand held tightly in mine, quietly watching the fire.

I commented, "This is indeed our celebration!—" and she silenced me with a kiss, lapsing back into my arms.

Sensing that she needed rest, I carried her to her bedroom and placed her on the bed. Covering her with a heavy blanket, I sat by her side caressing her cheeks. "Shortly I must return to the Widow's house. Coroner Houkyn and I are to leave for Reading at first light tomorrow, and I must pack for the trip. Were it not so, I would stay with you all night and keep you warm. The scare we had today made me appreciate how you have become very important to me in just a few weeks. I am in love with you, and hope you feel the same towards me!"

"Yes I do, Thomas! I want to be with you always. When you return from your trip, let us talk about making our future together. Now kiss me, and pat my head until I fall asleep. Full of hope and joy, I will await your return from Reading."

VII

SLEIGHT OF HAND

cs so

I AWAKENED BEFORE THE SUN on Monday and quickly packed my clothes and clerk's materials in a large, leather satchel, which would be tied behind the saddle on my traveling horse. Houkyn, aware that Bayardine was short-legged and would be unable to keep the pace he would set on his own steed, had directed me to rent a faster one from the livery stable. Having already ensured that this red-and-white roan was easy to ride, I walked the two blocks to the stable. The groom had had the horse fed and saddled by the time I arrived, and I was quickly on my way.

Coroner and clerk, dressed for the cold and wind, headed out on the road that would take us through the south gate. Our route would pass within six miles of my father's manor but veered off to the east and we with it. It initially went through an agricultural area of manors and farms with no significant town where we could stop to rest and water the horses.

Once under way, I decided that the time had come to mention to Houkyn what I had heard some days ago. "Sir, can we talk about something I unintentionally overheard from one of the other coroners, while I was reviewing the Coroners' Rolls?

The little bit of conversation, between coroner de Adynton and another man I had not seen previously, caused me to feel uncomfortable."

"Of course Thomas! Tell me what you heard and why it troubles you."

"The coroner and the man with him were talking about a large amount of money coming to de Adynton. I did not hear anything about why such a large sum would be coming his way. But I know that coroners are not paid—so the mention of a large sum of money caught my attention. I know that you and the other coroners have manors and can buy and sell goods and services, but I know from my father's manor that what he sells out of the crops harvested never produces significant payments to him. In a year it might amount to ten or twenty pounds, never a very large amount of money! Coroner de Adynton may be in a different situation than my father, and I am not accusing him of anything improper, but I felt it best to bring what I heard to your attention. You are probably more aware of his business dealings and can know if his sales of crops or other goods are likely to produce very large amounts of money."

Houkyn rode on for a couple of moments before he responded. "For all the time I have spent with him, I know little about his manors or his business transactions. I know he has three manors located in Oxfordshire and another in a neighboring shire. Beyond that, I know nothing of what he grows or raises on those manors or in what other business interests he is engaged. We Oxford coroners speak very little about matters beyond our coroner duties! I am hesitant about inquiring of him regarding "large sums of money" without some evidence of improper actions or dealings. If you hear anything more detailed regarding this large sum of money, please let me know."

For the next few miles nothing was said by either of us.

We made a few brief stops long enough to take care of personal needs and rest the horses but were into midday before we arrived in the town of Wallingford and found an inn with a watering trough. Tying up our mounts so they could drink, we went for something to eat. The innkeeper, a man named Issac Hough, greeted us. He said the inn didn't have food for travelers, only for guests, but seeing that Houkyn was a coroner from Oxford, he took us into the kitchen where he directed the cook to give us some cold sliced chicken and bread, along with cups of ale. We thanked him for his courtesy and gave him some silver as payment. The chicken was very tasty, and the ale revitalized us. Refreshed, we pushed on for the last ten miles to Reading.

The road from Wallingford was in better condition, and we quickly came upon others also traveling to Reading—one, a monk, was on his way to obtain medicines from the mother house of his order, and his traveling companion, an itinerant peddler, was going there to serve his regular customers in need of the small tools, sewing materials, and household items he carried from town to town. The peddler told us he had been in Oxford only four days prior and was traveling to manors and villages along the way. I asked if he had been to the manor of my father, Leoric Votary, south of Oxford.

"Not on this trip, but I visited his manor in late October and sold his housekeeper several small items for his household and other items to some of the peasants there. The manor was enjoying the fruits of a bountiful harvest, and all those to whom I sold things seemed well and satisfied with their lot in life."

I was happy to hear the news but wished we could have passed that way, if only for a brief visit. I missed my father and hoped he was well.

We continued southeast in a hurry because the sun was heading down, and the winds had begun to blow with a bit more force. Our horses, sensing our desire to finish the trip before darkness, picked up their pace to a brisk trot. We were able to reach Reading soon after the evening bells had rung out from the residence of the abbot. He lived just off the main road into town. We stopped to let him know of our arrival and to inquire about an inn where we might stay for two nights. The steward of the abbot's properties, aware that a coroner and clerk from Oxford were due in Reading that evening, informed us that the abbot had notified the innkeeper at the Reading Inn to expect us and had sent the innkeeper a purse of silver to pay for our lodging and food. We thanked him most warmly and asked that he convey our great appreciation to the abbot.

The innkeeper greeted us at the door. It was not often that the abbot sent guests to him, and he was eager to know what brought us to town. Not wanting word of our mission to be spread about, we told him we were in pursuit of a felon who had escaped the Oxford gaol. This appeared to satisfy his curiosity.

The innkeeper showed us to our room, which proved to be the finest in the establishment. "I am pleased to have such honorable gentlemen grace my inn with your presence. You must be tired from your long ride. I will have your horses wiped down and brushed, then given some grain. You, also, must be hungry? My cook is preparing a hot meal for you, as we speak. Once you have had time to refresh yourselves after your trip, please come down to the tavern, and he will serve you."

Houkyn replied, "We are overwhelmed by these accommodations, the comfortable room, the care for our horses, and a hot meal. You have our deepest appreciation. We will come downstairs forthwith to enjoy the meal your cook has prepared just for us."

We quickly removed our riding coats and washed up, to be seated and served slices of roast lamb with parsnips and carrots, accompanied by a locally made wine that proved better than expected. "What a fine meal!" Houkyn told the innkeeper. "It has been quite a long ride from Oxford, and we expected nothing better than some cold chicken and ale. I have never enjoyed a meal as much as this!"

We didn't linger at table, but asked the innkeeper to wake us early. Returning to our room and readying for bed, I could scarcely keep my eyes open long enough to get beneath the blanket; Houkyn took but a few moments longer before he too climbed into bed. We were asleep in moments.

Sometime during the night, I was awakened by a rustling sound, so soft that at first I thought it was my imagination playing tricks on me. I lay still, trying to go back to sleep, and then I heard it again. This time I was sure there was someone in the room, nearing our satchels, where Houkyn had hidden the king's gold coins.

I didn't believe that anyone but he and I could know our real reason for coming here or that we had the double leopards with us. I wanted to awaken Houkyn, but feared doing so would produce a startled utterance that would alert the prowler and allow him to escape. Instead, I listened carefully to determine more closely where he was in the room.

Eventually, I believed he was right near the window where we had placed our satchels and far enough from the door so that I could jump him and stop his escape. Slipping from the bed, I crawled towards him, hoping he would make a sound just loud enough that I would know exactly where he was. The sound came very soon, and I jumped at him while yelling for Houkyn to help me.

I landed on one of his legs and grabbed for his arms, all the while yelling. Houkyn piled in. For a while, my target seemed about to slip from my grip, but Houkyn was able to get his arm around the intruder's neck and held him tight. Seeing the coroner in control, I sought to light a candle, so we could see our captive and determine if he had been able to get anything from the satchels.

Before I could light the candle, a voice from the other side of the door demanded to know what was going on in our room and threatening to break down the door if we failed to open it immediately. I was happy to oblige and opened to find the innkeeper and his son, armed with knives and carrying candles. They entered, and I directed their attention to the person Houkyn had in his clutches.

The intruder, a young man, was unknown to us, but the innkeeper seemed to recognize him. Houkyn suggested that we take him downstairs to a room where we could interrogate him without disturbing other guests, an idea quickly agreed to by the innkeeper. His son took hold of the man, and with Houkyn in the lead and the innkeeper and me bringing up the rear, we descended to the main floor, into a small room, where the offender was secured to a chair.

"Young man! who are you, and what were you doing in our room?" Houkyn demanded. Getting no answer, he asked again, this time with his knife under the chin of our captive. Still no answer.

"Boy, this is the last time I will ask you. If you choose not to speak, I will have to turn you over to King Edward's gaolers. They have their ways of getting people to talk—painful ways!"

At that point, I turned to the innkeeper. "Sir, when you saw this man in our room, it appeared that you recognized him. Is that true? If so, will you identify him?"

The innkeeper was startled by my statement, and for a moment I feared I was mistaken. He cleared his throat and spoke up. "When I first saw this man, he looked familiar, but I was unable to recall where I might have seen him—and still am unable to put to him a name or a place where I saw him."

Houkyn again addressed the intruder. "I have grown impatient with your refusal to answer. I will give you one last chance to answer my questions. If you refuse, I will ask the abbot if I might throw you in his dungeon, to stay there at the king's pleasure, at which time his gaoler should bring you forth. His methods for getting answers will be exceeding painful. You would be wise to speak now, for after the king's men have their way, you may lack a tongue with which to speak!"

The young man's eyes showed his fear, and he began to sweat. At last he spoke. "My name be John. I entered your room in search of some coins that m'lord lost while in Oxford of late. He believes you have the coins. An' that you might return them to the king's mint, here in Reading. M'lord said it was urgent. I should get them straight this night or recovering them would be more difficult—or impossible! He promised to grant my freedom if I be successful. He has my wife and young son, an' he'll kill 'em should I fail! I fear him more than the king's gaolers. But naught matters to me now! I have failed and will never see my wife and child again in this world. Do with me as you will!—"

I thought I could see a look of hopelessness in his eyes, not of a thief but of a pawn in the hands of an evil man. I decided to plead for the youth and asked Houkyn to join me outside the room, and he agreed.

"Sir, what John has done is wrong, but given the threats to both himself and to his wife and child, I think he was doing what he could to save his family. He is also the link that could bring us the person who likely stole the gold coins from the king's mint. Perhaps we can use his assistance to get us close to his master. If he helps us—and the king's Reading mint—to capture his master, his assistance would justify forgiving his attempt, under duress, to get the coins from us."

The coroner looked into my eyes carefully. "And I suggest that we ask the innkeeper and his son to leave the room. I would not want to have our proposal to John be known to anyone else. Who knows whether either father or son has a connection to John's master."

"How do you suggest we ensure they not linger close to the door?"

"I shall use my position as Oxford coroner to firmly request that they go back to bed!" Whereupon Houkyn looked into the room and asked father and son to come out into the lobby, while I remained with John.

When they were well away, Houkyn drew them in close. Whispering, he told them that we needed more information from John and might need to get rough with him. He recommended they return to their beds and get some sleep, as only a few hours remained before they must open the inn. He promised to keep to a minimum the sounds of any beatings or other violence and preferred there be no witnesses to what might be done. Father and son were glad to be elsewhere, and both went back to their rooms quickly.

Houkyn returned and told John that he had committed a crime that could be punished quite severely. "John, while your behavior was wrong, we understand that you did it under threat from your master and not of your free will. We are interested in capturing your master, because he was the true thief of the coins. If you will assist us by telling us where we could find and arrest him, we would forgive your illegal behavior and help reunite you with your wife and child. We will never tell your master or anyone else that you helped us. We will also assist you in becoming a free man, no longer a vassal to your master, and able to offer your services to any willing to pay good money."

"What you have said you will do for me, in return for my help, is almost more than I could ever have hoped! But I am in great fear of my master, as I have seen him beat to death another vassal for spilling a pitcher of milk. I do want my freedom for myself and family, but I need your assurance that you will keep your end of such an agreement. Would you put what you've proposed to me in writing, which both you and I would sign as our agreement. If you do that, I will do all I can to help you capture my master!—"

Houkyn thought for a long moment and then agreed, to which he and John shook hands. "By tomorrow, Thomas will put our agreement into writing, so we both can sign. And once we have your master in this shire's gaol, we will give you a copy of our agreement to keep as protection for you and your family.

"And by the by, we told the innkeeper and son we would likely have to press you painfully—so as to encourage their disengagement. Do not forget to be in fear of us on their behalf!"

"Aye m'lord. You have treated me better than I deserve and offered a way to freedom for my family. I thank you from the bottom of my heart! Please now tell how I can assist you in capturing my master."

"First, we need to speak with the mint manager about the gold coins and try to determine how they were removed. It is not likely that the manager has any involvement in the taking of the coins, but not impossible. In the meantime, we will let you go back to your master with one or two of the gold coins and an explanation for why you don't have all ten. What do you think, Thomas?"

"He could say he was successful in slipping into our room and able to search for the coins without waking us, but there were only two in our satchels."

Houkyn liked the idea but thought John's master would question why we hadn't brought all ten coins with us. I suggested that we would have left eight of the coins in Oxford because we were concerned about the risk of being robbed along the road to Reading. The two coins would be sufficient to show the abbot and the master of the king's mint that we had all ten. And if we had been robbed, we would still have the other eight coins. We discussed this idea briefly before Houkyn agreed that it was a good explanation, adding with a smile, "Why did we not think of this aforehand, Thomas!"

"Good thing we were not robbed!" I replied, and he sent me back to our room to get two double leopards.

The coins in hand, Houkyn reviewed with John the explanation he would give his master. When both were satisfied of the gambit, he asked John for directions to the manor, located west of Reading, and the master's proper name, Antoine de Glissaude, who had arrived here several years before from France, where his father was a prominent landowner. It was said he had purchased the manor for a pittance.

We quietly escorted John out of the inn before anyone awoke and came downstairs. The sun was rising, so we took the remaining eight coins, leaving a note for the innkeeper saying we had removed our prisoner, but we would return within a few hours.

Once away a fair distance, we sent John off to the manor and continued on to the king's mint nearby. We were curious to see the security and tried to take note of all the protective measures employed. When we were admitted to the mint, I noticed that the entrance was a solid wooden door that opened outward, with metal brackets where a stout wooden crosspiece was inserted to prevent the door from opening.

The man who admitted us was just one of the workers, not a mint official, so I asked if he was the regular doorkeeper. He shook his head and told me the doorkeeper was whomever was nearest to the door when the bell was rung for admittance. He escorted us to the manager of the mint, Edward Bellemere, then returned to his work.

"Thank you, Mr. Bellemere, for agreeing to meet with us! My name is Arthur Houkyn. I am the chief coroner for the town of Oxford and this is my clerk, Thomas Votary. I sent a messenger to you last week, to say that during an investigation at the site of a murder we recovered a pouch containing several of the king's newly minted but not yet released gold double leopards. We had heard that the king had directed his several mints of the realm to begin minting those coins, but his royal highness was awaiting an auspicious occasion to give the order formally to issue these new and special coins.

"We have come to return the coins we have in our possession and to advise you that we have learned that these coins had been stolen. Of all the king's mints, the only one even close to Oxford is here. We have assumed that the gold coins we recovered at the murder site most likely were stolen from this mint. Were you aware, prior to receiving my message, that any coins have been removed from this mint without your knowledge?"

"Coroner Houkyn, your message came as a total surprise! You are correct that this mint is producing the new double leopards, but we believe that we have all of the double leopards we have minted secure in a location under double lock and key, as you might say! We question your assumption that this mint has been robbed. Those leopards must have come from another royal mint."

"Sir, since our arrival here in Reading, we have learned that the person who was carrying the coins when they were lost in Oxford lives within a few miles of where we stand. His close proximity to this mint suggests that this is indeed where those coins were taken."

"Sir Arthur Houkyn, I am not convinced that your assumption is correct, but I would be a fool not to consider it. I will immediately order a count of the double leopards we have minted and secured in the vault."

"Your action is a prudent one! I trust that you will allow us to observe the count?"

"But of course. It is your good work trying to restore the coins to us and detecting who was in possession of them when they were lost. I welcome you to observe and to speak up should you see anything suggesting a miscount. We will secure the entrance to the mint immediately, then call all workers concerned together to inform them of the need to do an immediate recount of the double leopards in the mint's possession."

He acted as he had spoken. His deputy manager promptly went to close the entrance and insert the wooden bar. Next the deputy went to each workplace and asked those working there to come to the counting room immediately. An assistant called the roll of those assembled and finally proclaimed, "Sir, all are present."

Bellemere stepped forward and told his workers that information had come to him suggesting that there may be fewer double leopards in the strong-room than the mint's records say are here. "We will do a count of the number of these coins in each of our storage boxes. I will divide you into pairs, and each pair will count the coins in the storage box placed before you. One person of each pair will count out loud, and the other person will record a mark on paper for each ten coins counted. We will collect the papers from each pair of counters and add up the numbers from all the papers. The total should match the number of coins we have recorded in our records. We will do a second count of each box, to be done by a different set of counters. I will now select the people who will be paired as counters. Be aware that these two gentlemen who have joined us for the count and my assistant and I will be keeping a close eye on the counting. If any of you feel that your partner is not properly counting or keeping track, raise your hand."

He then selected the men to be paired and sent them to one of the counting tables to begin. Houkyn and I moved closer to the tables and agreed which tables each would watch. Bellemere and his assistant did the same.

The first counts went quickly, but I saw nothing that suggested any impropriety. Bellemere then paired new sets of counters and assigned each to count a box that neither had counted during the first round. The second count went as quickly as the first, and the totals for each box were recorded. Bellemere asked us and his assistant to retire to the far corner of the room to compare the totals of each count to be sure the numbers were the same—as they proved to be. He then asked that I add up the totals from each box. My grand total was then compared to his ledger.

He dismissed the workers for the day. Next he revealed to us that there was a difference of ten double leopards between his ledger and today's count. "I apologize for doubting you about the theft of coins from our mint. You were correct, there are ten missing! The gold coins you recovered must have, in some way, been taken from this mint."

Houkyn then asked Bellemere if there had ever been visitors who were shown through the mint, including any places where the minted coins might have been on view. "I suspect that one or more visitors who were given a tour of the mint had opportunity to handle some of the coins and had used a sleight of hand to palm and drop them into an inside pocket or hidden purse. Have you or your assistant ever escorted an important guest through the mint and perhaps allowed that person a bit more opportunity to slip a coin off the table?"

"We have had occasional visitors, often crown officials sent here by the king and, less often, visitors who were local lords or other prominent individuals interested in seeing how the coins of the realm are minted."

Houkyn inquired if he or his assistant could recall the

names of any of the visitors, particularly ones from the area around Reading. "I assume that the crown officials were here on royal business and showed their credentials to you. I am more interested in those visitors from this area, especially those who otherwise had no business interest with the mint. Would you and your assistant prepare a list of visitors from this immediate area?"

"We should be able to have a list by tomorrow at midday. You have done us a great service in calling to our attention the theft of those coins and bringing back those you recovered in Oxford."

Reminded by Bellemere's last few words, Houkyn produced the pouch of eight coins in our possession, counted out six for safekeeping and explained that the rest must be kept in evidence. The mint master thanked us both, but we noticed he looked faintly disappointed.

It had been a long day, following the long ride of the previous day and the overnight capture of John in our room. I was looking forward to a good dinner at the inn and a full night of sleep. Houkyn thanked Bellemere for the very thorough method of counting the coins, which guaranteed that there would be an accurate count, and we took our leave.

As we walked back to the inn, we wondered whether John would live up to his promise to help us catch his master.

When we arrived at the inn, we immediately headed to the dining room and ordered a bottle of wine. As we sat and drank the wine, the innkeeper came to our table to ask what we would like to eat. He said the cook was making a roast of pork and chicken with dumplings. Houkyn ordered the pork while I had the chicken. After an important agreement with John, and a bit of good detective work at the mint, I felt that we had earned this respite of good food, wine and an opportunity to relax. As I ate my meal, I felt a sense of exhaustion coming over me, and observed that Houkyn's eyelids looked heavy. I told him that I had to go to bed soon or someone would need to carry me up to our room. He nodded in agreement.

The climb to our room took all my energy to complete. In the room at last, we threw off our clothes and I stumbled into bed. Houkyn was enough awake to prop a chair against the door, before he too got into bed.

We slept until nearly prime, and even when I awoke my body kept telling me to go back to sleep. But Houkyn urged me to get up, as we had much to do today. Most important would be the return of John to report on his master's response. Would the lord of the manor be suspicious that his vassal might have found more than two but kept the rest for himself? We had asked John to meet us halfway between the town and the manor at about three hours past prime, by the bells of terce; he had told us of a large tree on the trail.

We went down to the dining room in hopes of finding something to eat, but there was nothing available, so we returned to our room to get our coats before heading into Reading's village center in search of food. A cold breeze was blowing, but nothing was going to deter us from breaking our fast. We were in the middle of the village, when we overheard a conversation about a body that had been found just west of town this morning. We looked at one another, wondering if it was John. Much as I wanted to follow the path towards John's master's manor to learn whether it was his body, we needed to avoid seeming to have an interest in this death.

It didn't take long before word was being circulated on the streets as to the name of the deceased. Whether truth or rumor, it was not John. The story that accompanied the name was of was a young man from a nearby village who had been seeing a married woman behind her husband's back. The husband becoming suspicious of his wife's frequent, unexplained absences from their cottage, had hidden nearby to see where she went.

The gist was this: Within a short time of his "departure" from the cottage, ostensibly to do some work for a friend who lived a mile away, the husband spied his wife leaving the house. He followed at a distance and soon saw her meet up with the young man, whom she kissed most passionately. The couple then went on to the young man's house. The husband went to a window and saw the two in bed engaged in licentious behavior. He waited behind some trees until his wife emerged and she headed towards home. A moment later the young man emerged and took the path towards Reading. The husband picked up a fair-size rock and followed. When the pursued stopped to relieve himself, the husband struck him on the head several times.

How all of this became known to any of the story spreaders was unclear, and some or all could be made up by anyone who did not like the husband. Houkyn and I chose to wait until the undersheriff returned from the scene and from his conversation with the dead man's wife and reported what he had learned from his inquiries. But what we heard on the street didn't match up with what we knew about John, his wife and son.

While we and others awaited the undersheriff's report, we decided to return to the mint to thank the manager for the very thorough manner in which he had determined the missing gold coins. We also wanted to learn if he and his assistant had been able to compile a list of locals who had been given tours of the mint. But not before breaking our fast.

The mint manager received us warmly and thanked us again. He was anxious to recover all of the coins before one of the king's men came back to inform the mint of the date on which the new coins were to be released for circulation. We tried to reassure him that we were also in pursuit of the person who had purloined those coins, and hoped in the next day to have more information.

"Master Bellemere, have you been able to make a list of persons?"

"We have, Sir Arthur, most of it from memory. Let me get it from my desk."

He had a single sheet of paper with no more than a dozen names on it.

"This is very helpful! Can you tell me where each of these men lives, and what is their business or other source of income?"

"I will ask my assistant to join us, as he knows some of these men better than I."

They returned in a moment, and Bellemere introduced his assistant as Robert d'Antonio.

Houkyn began the discussion by telling them that there was a reasonable chance that the thief of the double leopards resided within five miles of Reading. "The more we know about each person on your list, the greater the likelihood that we can narrow down our investigation to just one or a couple of the people on the list. Let us begin with the first person on the list, Donal Johnson. Robert, you apparently know more about him. Where does he live?"

"He resides in Reading and is the headmaster at the village academy. He came to visit in September, and I invited him to see how we mint coins. The new gold piece was the coin we had just begun to mint only a week before his visit. He was most interested in how we made the gold disks that would be stamped to create the front and back of the resulting coins. He had assumed that we began by melting gold and then pouring it into the mold. We told him that the gold disks, which we refer to as "blanks," are soft enough that we didn't need to melt the gold. The weight of the stamper, and the softness of the gold disks enabled us to produce the front and back at the same time by using a very heavy die attached to the stamping device. I gave him a blank to hold, and after he returned it, we placed it in the stamping device. We then gave the disk two solid hits of the stamper.

"When I removed the disk, he was amazed to see that it now had the front and back royal marks stamped upon it—the symbolic mark of the king flanked by leopards on the front and the royal cross with more leopards on the reverse. He told me that he would make what he had just seen the subject of a lecture he would give to the most advanced class at the academy."

Houkyn asked, "Was there any time during his tour when he might have been able to secretly slip one or more of the coins into his pocket?"

"No, I was with him during the entire tour and never saw his hand close to a coin, just the unstamped gold blank."

Houkyn then turned to Bellemere and asked about the second name on the list. "What can you tell us about John Spencer?"

Bellemere proceeded to tell us that Spencer was the lord of a manor just outside of Reading to the northwest. "He had visited the mint in early October and said that some of the villeins working on his manor had found what appeared to be nuggets of gold. He was interested in knowing whether he could pay us to use the mint's coin-making equipment to make his own coins. I had to inform him that the mint was for the sole use of minting the new gold coins designed and ordered by King Edward III. I would have loved to have his business, as the mint is often idle for lack of orders from the king. He was disappointed but accepted the king's purpose for this mint. He asked if he might see the remainder of the coin-making process, just in case he found himself with a large number of gold nuggets and wanted to set up his own mint. We were happy to oblige."

Houkyn then asked whether Lord Spencer might have had an opportunity to palm one or more of the coins during his tour.

Bellemere thought for a moment and then told us that Spencer had suffered a coughing spell near the end of the tour and seemed to be temporarily incapacitated by the coughing. "I asked if I could bring him some water to drink. I went to fetch the water, but when I returned Spencer seemed to have recovered. We continued the tour, and near the end he suffered another coughing spell. Again I went for water, but he was fully recovered when I returned. He thanked me profusely for trying to assist him and said that he had experienced coughing fits a few times before but never like that day. He was able to climb the stairs to the exterior door and walk away from the mint without assistance. I had given no thought about the coins, which were in a box only a short distance away, on the other side of the room, but your question and the answer I just gave—have caused me to wonder if the fits of coughing were nothing more than a diversion."

Houkyn looked to me and nodded, indicating that Spencer had become his primary suspect.

I nodded in return and asked Bellemere about the next name on his list. We proceeded to ask questions about each, but nothing we heard of them aroused further suspicion. We tried not to let on that Spencer had become a suspect. Now we needed to speak with John and learn how his master had reacted.

We took our leave from Bellemere and d'Antonio and started back towards the inn, but before we had gone fifty yards I raised a concern. "What if one or both of the men we just left are involved in the theft of the gold coins? Should I find a location where I can observe the mint's exit door and watch to see if either of them leaves and goes towards the path that runs towards the manor where John is a villein. They might want to warn the manor owner that we are closing in on him."

Houkyn agreed with my keeping an eye on their activities. "They may be in league with Spencer or willing to play him against us, whichever works to their advantage!"

I walked back towards the mint, all the while looking for a place where I might watch for them without freezing. Nothing lent itself to my purpose until within about fifty yards of the mint, I spotted a small tavern with windows on two sides, one facing the mint. I entered and asked the server for an ale. That I could sit and watch the mint's exit while enjoying an ale proved better than expected. I settled back to watch. At least an hour had passed, and I had begun to think I was wasting my time. The server asked if I wanted another ale, and just as I was about to say no, I saw the mint's assistant manager come out, look about as if searching for someone, and then walk quickly in a westerly direction. I left the server a silver groat, and quickly exited the tavern.

D'Antonio occasionally looked to his left and then his right, but he never turned around. He walked on for more than a mile, then turned left onto a narrow path westerly. The narrowness of the trail, while making it more difficult for me to see him, made it as difficult to look back and see me. As a result, I was able to stay no more than twenty yards behind him. At last we stopped. He looked about, turned right, and pushed through a dense patch of high grass, very dry from recent cold weather. Just beyond was another, wider trail, and he took the left branch of it. Able to walk more rapidly on this trail, he began to pull away from me, and I needed to pick up my pace to keep him in sight. At last he slowed, and I could see ahead of us an open area and evidence of harvested fields.

Clearly, this was a manor. D'Antonio looked about before continuing on the trail, which ran along the southern border of the fields and probably was used during the planting and harvesting seasons by the manor's villeins to and from the fields. With little to hide behind, I dropped back further and used any trees and bushes to stay hidden. Houkyn had been clear before agreeing to following either of the mint officials; I was to observe, not to be seen. I stopped behind brush for cover and a good view across the fields towards the manor house.

The last I saw of d'Antonio was him entering the impressive house. I waited a good while to see if he would emerge, but when he didn't, I turned and followed the trail back to Reading. Because the sun, already dim, was near the horizon, I picked up my pace to a dogtrot and was back before sunset.

I went directly to the inn, expecting Houkyn to be there or to find a message, but there was neither. I settled into a chair in the entry area to await his return. The innkeeper came to the front desk and greeted me. He had not seen Houkyn since the morning but assured me he would likely return soon, as the temperature dropped and darkness took over the sky. He asked if I would care for an ale or some wine, and I agreed to another ale. It arrived quickly, and I settled in until Houkyn returned a short time later. He was surprised when I told him of Robert d'Antonio's long walk to the west of Reading, to the manor. I couldn't prove that the manor belonged to John's master, but it appeared to be located approximately where he had described it.

"This is turning into something much larger than we could have imagined when we found the pouch of gold coins only a few weeks ago. Instead of a robbery from the mint, it is beginning to look like a conspiracy between John's master and the assistant mint director to smuggle some of the new double leopard gold coins from the mint. If coins are removed from the mint until next summer and the conspiracy not exposed, the number of coins taken could be in the hundreds. If Bellemere and d'Antonio are both involved, the number of coins they have been recording each week may be substantially below the actual production. Had we not found the pouch of coins at the murder scene, it is likely no one would have become aware of this scheme, and the king might never have discovered the crime."

"What should we do with what we are learning? To whom can we turn to bring this to the attention of the king?"

"A coroner can bring this to the attention of His Majesty, though we are working outside of our designated territory, the town of Oxford. The alternative would be to bring what we've learned to the sheriff of Oxfordshire. I have reservations about this latter option. The Oxfordshire sheriff has a reputation for profiteering from matters in which he becomes involved. He might want a share of what the mint's manager and assistant are stealing. I think we ought to bring the evidence directly to the king's attention—once we hear back from John."

I was worried about John. We were expecting to hear from him before now. Then a sickening thought occurred. I told Houkyn where our plan might have a significant flaw. "Sire, when we gave the six gold coins to Bellemere, we may have put John in grave danger. When I followed him, d'Antonio was probably going to the manor to report that we had returned six of the coins. His lordship may have begun to doubt John's excuse for finding only two—"

"You make an interesting point! But a logical explanation may be that we had hidden the other eight coins elsewhere in the room or under lock and key at the innkeeper's desk."

Houkyn was right, as far as it went, but John had still not come back, and that kept my concern alive. "Sire, is there anything we could do to require John's master to send him to Reading? Is there anyone of authority that could direct his master to send John to him for questioning, perhaps regarding an attempted robbery at the inn, or for another reason?"

"An interesting idea! That manor, like others, is surely a subdivision of a hundred, which is a subdivision of the county. The bailiff of the hundred is its chief law enforcement official. I believe that the bailiff of the hundred in this part of the county has his office in Reading. I'll make a discrete inquiry of the mayor of Reading to learn his name and the location of his office."

Putting thought into action, Houkyn left the inn and went looking for the mayor. Though it is a good-size town, Reading is not so large that it took very long to locate the office, just as the man was getting ready to leave for the day. Houkyn introduced himself as the head coroner of Oxford, trying to solve a crime that had produced evidence that made it necessary to come to the mayor's town. He needed to find the bailiff for this hundred. Could the mayor direct him?

Not used to hearing about murders in distant towns or their connection to his town, the mayor was interested in more details, but Houkyn told him that he could not divulge such, until the case came to trial, lest he get in trouble with the judges of the Oxfordshire county court.

Reassured by this insight into the law, the mayor directed him three buildings down to the left, where he would find the bailiff, Judah Mallory.

Soon thereafter, Houkyn was admitted by the bailiff himself. Identifying his position and reason for coming to Reading, the coroner quickly explained the need to question a villein named John, who lived on a manor a couple of miles to the west. He asked if the bailiff might be able to issue a summons or other legally binding directive to the lord of that manor, directing him to send this man John—accompanied by the person who delivers the directive—back to Reading for questioning. It would be helpful, Houkyn added, if the messenger would tell his lordship that John is not a suspect, but may be able to provide information about a suspect in an attempted robbery.

Judah Mallory was an affable fellow. "I see no reason why I couldn't dispatch my assistant to present Antoine de Glissaude, Lord of Longate Manor—the same where John is a villain—with a bailiff's summons directing his lordship to send the said John to said bailiff for such questioning!

"I know his lordship and do not think him honorable, but I have not enough to prove any offence and will be happy to send such a summons first thing tomorrow morning. I'll make no reference to you as the person requesting the presence of this John, and will send it with a very able assistant. If you will return in the early afternoon, I expect that John will be here awaiting your arrival."

VIII

JOHN'S STORY

C３ ８Ｃ

H OUKYN, PLEASED WITH BAILIFF MALLORY and his attitude towards Lord de Glissaude, returned to the inn and joined me in the front room, where I was enjoying more of the local ale. He told me of Mallory's quick and positive response. "Your idea proved to be our way to see John without his master—presumably de Glissaude and not Spencer! You have, once again, impressed me with your quick and pertinent thinking, Thomas!"

"Thank you, sir! I know that a clerk has very specific duties that don't include trying to be a coroner, but when I think I can help you resolve a problem or offer a different way of looking at evidence, I hope you will consider it on its merits, not just on who offers it to you. I will try, always, to be discreet, and want you to consider it your own if you wish to speak of it to your fellow coroners."

The sounds and aromas coming from the kitchen told our stomachs that it was time to adjourn to the dining room. We sought a table off to one side, to discuss what we had learned so far and to plan what questions to ask of John—including any fictions for the Lord of Longate to hear when John returned.

The innkeeper stopped at our table and welcomed us back.

He told us the main courses on offer this evening were bœuf bourguignon and pork loin with leeks. We both chose the beef, an item I seldom had during my time living in Oxford. Once again the meal was very good, and we asked our host to convey our enjoyment to the cook.

Since we wanted to convince de Glissaude that John was not a suspect, we came up with the name Orvyn Barber for a suspect and decided that he was from a little village away from the River Thames, east of Reading, far enough that his lordship was unlikely to have any familiarity.

Then we needed a reason why the suspect had been in Reading on the day and night when John had tried to rob us. Because his last name was Barber, it would likely be his occupation. We decided he was a traveling barber, going from town to town, cutting hair where there was no resident barber. He was only passing through Reading for the night before going on to his next destination north. As a traveling barber he didn't make much money but had learned to keep his eyes and ears open for other less savory opportunities that might yield a better return. He was soon gone from anyplace where he had benefited from one of those other opportunities, before anyone was aware. In this case, he had overheard that an important man was staying at the inn; Barber was suspected of entering an unlocked room late at night and searching a satchel for something of good value. He didn't find anything worth stealing and went to another room, but the persons in that room woke up.

John was in the vicinity and joined the traditional "hue and cry" set up by the innkeeper. While he was not one of the men who captured Orvyn Barber, he announced that he had seen Barber lurking close to the inn a short while before the hue and cry was sounded. He had also helped run the barber to ground. John was being questioned to learn more about what he had seen regarding the person captured. We were pleased with the story, thus far, and on the next morning sought out Bailiff Mallory to get his thoughts on whether de Glissaude would likely believe that someone other than his villein had been arrested.

Mallory thought it devilishly interesting to fool his lordship, and he suggested a few minor changes to the story. We liked them well enough, and the deputy bailiff, necessarily taken into confidence, would deliver the tale later this day, returning with John the villein, who lived in hope of safety for his family and freedom from bondage. Mallory drafted the summons with wording to reinforce the false narrative.

Upon his arrival, the deputy bailiff presented himself to de Glissaude's butler, stated his purpose in brief, and asked to see his lordship on bailiff's business. The butler was gone several minutes, then returned to escort him to the lord's work room, where he was introduced.

"I understand you have a message for me from Bailiff Mallory. Please present it!"

"M'lord, here is a summons for your villein John to come with me to provide the bailiff with such information as John has regarding his ability to identify a man captured for attempting to rob guests at the Reading Inn earlier this week. Bailiff Mallory respectfully requests that you send John with me to Reading, where he will be asked to make a statement regarding what he saw that night. The bailiff states that John is not a suspect, and faces no charges."

As planned, the deputy said no more than absolutely necessary, just enough that John might catch on if questioned by de Glissaude alone. The rest of the story was ready if needed. If John were present to agree, all the better.

Lord Glissaude read the written summons, thought for a moment. "Yes, I will send my butler to find John, and you may take him to Reading to provide his testimony." What the assistant bailiff did not observe was the very curious smile that crept across the lord's face.

The butler returned a short time later with John, who wisely kept his mouth shut. The assistant bailiff thanked the lord of the manor and departed with John for Reading. They traveled quickly on the frozen trail and were in town well before sunset. They went immediately to the bailiff's office, where they found

Mallory and Houkyn telling stories about their experiences as part of the legal system, such as it was and is, in the long struggle for fairness and equity where the common law proves inflexible.

Houkyn was quick to rise and greet John again, much relieved and most interested in learning about de Glissaude's reaction to the story about robbing us of the two gold coins.

Mallory's curiosity was for more local reasons—the shady activities associated with the manor, on which John might be able to shed light. The deputy got the rest of the day off, mostly to reward his service in getting John back to Reading but also because there were things he wished to hear from John that should remain confidential, at least for the time being.

I arrived just as Houkyn and Mallory were preparing to talk with John, and they invited me to join them. Houkyn took the lead in the conversation. "How did you fare when you returned to your manor early the morning after you "visited" our room at the inn? Did your master accept that there were but two of the ten gold coins in our satchels?"

"He weren't pleased, sire—that I could find but two leopards. He raved on about your cunning, to put the others in another place—under lock and key at the inn. I think he took you for mere messengers from the Oxford coroner, not the chief coroner himself, an' he couldn't believe that a messenger would be smart enough to hide the rest of 'em."

Houkyn, Mallory and I heartily enjoyed John's retelling of some of his lordship's unrestrained comments, and John joined in the laughter.

"Did he ever ask you what else you did at the inn that night?"

"No!—sire. He appeared to accept that what I was able to take was all could be found in your room and that I stayed in town until morning, it being too hard to follow the trail to the manor in the dark. He thinks I'm but a dolt, unable to fool him. An' I try to keep it so in his mind!"

"Did he say anything about wanting to try to regain the other eight coins?"

"No, sire. He talks about such activities only with his manor steward. He wants no one else to know his dishonest goings-on—but for his steward. They conspires together."

"Have you ever heard how he came to lose the ten double leopards in Oxford town?"

"He did not intend for me to hear his tale, but I was working in the manor house, near his private work room, when he spoke of it with the steward. It was a mild day for the season, and his door was open a crack to let in some air. He said he had gone to Oxford town to meet the owner of some manors in Oxfordshire, a man he had done business with before. He intended to seek the man's help in bringing a large number of leopards from the Reading mint to Oxford."

"Did he say why he would bring them to Oxford?"

"In a way!—sire, m'lud. He said Oxford has such an amount of trade with other countries that the coins would be easier to exchange for older coins—or for other goods, in Oxford. And the distance from Reading was not far, but far enough not to be where anyone would think they had traveled. He told his steward that there were more leopards to be had, and no one would know which mint they came from. Many more!—sire. He needs a partner in Oxford who knows the kinds of folk who would be willing to carry them to other parts of the realm and France, an' the Italian states, an' beyond. Someone who already does trading in a variety of goods."

"We became aware of the ten gold coins while investigating a murder near the Oxford University student community. The early evidence made us think that the dead man had been killed to get the coins, but I am now beginning to think that he may have been following your master—or someone—because he somehow knew that person was carrying some of the yet-to-be released coins, and he intended to steal them. Did you ever hear about that Oxford incident?"

"Nothing—sire! Only that something happened, and he lost the pouch with the coins."

At that point, Mallory asked, "Can you tell us of any dishonest deals or schemes in which he is presently involved?"

John thought for a moment. "I don't know of anything particular, but have heard bits of talk that he has met with a banker from Florence, a city-state, they say, when the lord and the banker lately were both in London. Some sort of money scheme."

Mallory said to John that if he learned any more about any of de Glissaude's schemes, he would be most interested in any information John might provide, but he didn't want John to put himself at risk. "You have been very helpful with what you've told us about your master. If ever I can help you towards your freedom and a better life for you, your wife and child—just say the word!"

"Thank you, sire! And I will listen carefully when I am around his lordship and let you know if I hear something."

Houkyn then turned our attention to preparing John for questions that de Glissaude might upon John's return from "giving evidence." At some length we rehearsed what responses he could provide as to what he supposedly told Bailiff Mallory— until we all felt confident of the Orvyn Barber story.

Houkyn said, finally, "John, you have done well. Lord de Glissaude should believe your responses. Thomas and I must return to Oxford, where we'll pursue the lead you suggested about your lord wanting a partner with experience in trade and contacts beyond Oxfordshire. Before this matter is resolved, I anticipate that we will need to return to Reading. My hope is that you and your family will be able accompany us to Oxford the next time, free of any obligation to the Lord of Longate and be able to make a new life in our fine city."

We returned to the inn, retrieved our satchels and horses, bid farewell and settled up with the innkeeper. We were fortunate to have good weather for our travel and made good time. Our horses, inactive for several days, were glad of the opportunity. The sun warmed us while we rode.

IX

MARK OF THE MASTER

CB   EO

A FTER A FEW MILES OF riding, I broke the silence by returning to a subject I had raised with Houkyn on our
trip to Reading. "Sir, do you recall our brief discussion about
what I had unintentionally overheard spoken between Coroner
de Adynton and the unnamed man?"

"It was about a large amount of money that was supposedly
coming to de Adynton. Are you thinking what I am thinking?"

"About Lord de Glissaude's reported desire to find someone
in Oxford with experience—"

"De Adynton might well be the kind of person Lord de
Glissaude wants to assist him in getting the purloined gold
coins distributed around the realm and beyond."

We rode on in silence, and I waited until Houkyn resumed
his thoughts aloud. "Ricard de Adynton certainly has experience
in trade, and has manors not only in Oxfordshire, but in at
least one other shire, if not more. He occasionally mentions
his travels, and has more than once mentioned journeying to
such places as London, York, Norwich, Bristol, and Lincoln.
But many others engage in trade, and travel long distances to
trade their goods and crops. Is there something more specific

you learned in Reading that leads you to think he might be in league with Antoine de Glissaude?"

"There is no single bit of information that leads me to consider him. But the fact that the pouch of gold coins was found in Oxford leads me to wonder who in our town Lord de Glissaude, presumably, was going to meet, when he was confronted, as we surmise, by the person now dead. Could that person he was to meet be Coroner de Adynton, a lord who could operate under cover of the law?"

"The Oxford connection seems strong, but we know nothing about the man who was talking with de Adynton at our meeting room. If we could find a way to identify him, it would go a long way towards determining if there is a link between de Adynton and our de Glissaude."

"Indeed. But I have no relationship with de Adynton other than being clerk for the Oxford coroners. He would have no reason to respond to my questions. I wish I had seen Lord de Glissaude while we were in Reading!"

"I don't have much of a relationship with him either, but it is better than yours. I will think about how I might initiate a discussion. It is complicated, because only you were present when the "money" comment was made by de Adynton's visitor."

"Indeed! I, too, will think about a way to learn the visitor's name." Then it struck me, "Sir Thomas, it may not be as important to know his name, if we know who would know that we were on this case and traveling to Reading to be robbed."

"Ah, Thomas, my clerk, that does narrow it down to a coroner in the room, when we planned our trip to the mint! More weight to the possible guilt of the one who talked to another of large amounts of coin."

The rest of our ride was uneventful, and we reached the town's south gate before the sun set. I returned the roan at the livery stable, and walked quickly back to the Widow Rowley's house, arriving in time to join my fellow tenants for the evening meal. They wanted to know all about my trip. I dwelt on our travel there and back and spun the tale of the attempted robbery of two guests staying at the same inn, the hue and cry made by the innkeeper, and the eventual capture of the thief.

Unfortunately, they were drawn in all the more and demanded to know every detail of the crime. I had to come up with many more details than Houkyn and I had developed for John. I felt increasingly badly about my deception but was not sure why. Was I also a liar? Would I next be a cheat like the others? Was I untrustworthy, giving away a story tangential to my responsibilities as coroner's clerk? Where was the reality in all this telling? At last, Margaret Rowley rescued me by diverting their attention, offering glasses of her homemade wine. They all accepted, and the conversation shifted to how she was able to make it taste so good. I was much relieved, as I was running out of ideas, not to mention self-respect!

I pleaded exhaustion and retired to my room. Just before I climbed into bed, I spotted a slip of paper on the table next to it. On it was a note from Rebecca, in her crude scrawl, saying how much she missed me and asking that I come to see her as soon as possible. Doing so was already my intent, but her request had a sense of urgency, and I decided to visit her house early next morning, before she went to work.

I was asleep within an instant, slept soundly all night, and awoke with the sun. I quickly dressed, took a slice of bread with butter, ran out the door and didn't stop until I was at Rebecca's door. I knocked twice and was rewarded. Barely awake, it took a moment for her to realize it was me in the doorway. She let out a cry of happiness and threw her arms about my neck while kissing me deeply. Then she stopped suddenly and demanded to know why I had been gone so long. "I've been waiting days for your return—and missing you! I thought you could be dead!"

"Rebecca, I do apologize for not returning sooner, but my work as the coroner's clerk—" She put her hand over my mouth, kissed my cheek, and led me into the warmth of the kitchen.

"But I am back now," I protested with pleasure, "and later today, after you finish work, I have something important to discuss with you—you forgive me?"

"Yes I will, Thomas! And now you are fishing. But I, too, have something I need to discuss with you. Let us meet here at nine hours past prime, at the bells of nones, as I will be home by then."

"I will be here, with bells on!" Then the next kiss came and a hug, and I headed back to the Widow's to break my fast before going to the coroners' meeting room. Alfred was eating a piece of bread and drinking hot tea. I poured myself some tea, sliced a piece of his mother's homemade bread, and joined him. We talked about events in Oxford during my absence and a little about my trip. Then I thought to ask him about who in Oxford was largely involved in trade. I didn't want to have my question interpreted as part of my work, so I prefaced by talking about my father's interest in finding a trader who might help him earn more from his manorial crops. "Alfred, you know Oxford much better than I. Who are the major traders who live here in town or nearby and have trading routes that go far afield?"

He thought about it, munching the thickly buttered bread, and began listing those who were deeply involved in such trade. "The most prominent of the Oxford trading companies belongs to a cousin of King Edward, named Robert Benjamin. He trades in wool, wine, and wheat; he is known to travel to the states of the Hanseatic League, a union of several German coastal cities, and other commercial cities of the Baltic region. The Hanse has been granted special privileges in England and has as its chief post the so-called Steelyard in London. Another major trading company is owned by Donal d'Italien, who specializes in trading with the city-states of northern Italy, with Florence and Venice the major commercial cities. Those states have long had trading ties with commercial cities throughout the Mediterranean region, and through those cities they have access to the Orient.

A third major trader is Bertrand Marchand, who trades in grains, wool and precious metals. He does much of his trading with the Low Countries, particularly in Flanders, which has become a very important trade center for the English. The

Low Countries have no armies, but their commercial naval fleets provide transportation for other trading countries and commercial cities throughout the region. They trade for themselves, but also transport goods for other countries and traders, acting as middlemen.

Lastly, is one of your coroners, Ricard de Adynton, who trades in grains, wool and precious metals. He grows large amounts of several varieties of grain, raises large flocks of longhair sheep, and has connections with traders in the Low Countries, and in parts of France, which are, or previously were, under English rule. I don't know where or with whom he trades precious metals, but those are valuable commodities in every trading center, of course. I don't believe he has any precious metal mines on his manors in Oxfordshire or in Buckinghamshire, where he has his largest manor, in the village of Marlow. Of these four major traders, your father's most promising partner would probably be de Adynton."

I thanked him and commended him for his knowledge. I promised to share his information with my father and to recommend de Adynton as the one most likely to be interested in his crops. Another lie. Then I left for the coroners' meeting room, hoping to find Houkyn there—alone.

He was there, but so was Coroner Morcant de Whatele, so I set up my writing materials and began to make notes of my conversation with Alfred, before I forgot much of what he told me. I was excited with the information, which I feared might lead to forgetfulness.

A long while later, de Whatele announced to Houkyn that he was leaving for the day in order to take care of personal business and would be back in a few days. I allowed the room to get quiet after his departure. Then I blurted out, "Sir, the four major commercial traders living in Oxford, or in the suburbs around Oxford, are Robert Benjamin, Donal d'Italien, Bertrand Marchand and," I paused until he was looking straight at me, "Ricard de Adynton." I told him what I had learned from Alfred regarding the types of trading goods in which each specialized and the countries in which they did much of their trade. "We think of de Adynton's commercial activities as based in Oxford, because he has several manors within a few miles of here, but his largest manor is not in Oxfordshire, it is in Buckinghamshire, in the village of Marlow." I then repeated, "One of the areas where he does much of his trading is in those parts of France under English rule or which have been under English rule. He travels to those areas regularly to trade his goods."

It was suddenly clear to me that if Alfred knew the names of the major traders, Coroner Houkyn probably knew them personally. But he simply replied, "Explain to me why you believe his trading in areas of France now or formerly controlled by England has anything to do with our investigation."

"As you may recall, Lord de Glissaude is originally from a part of France under English rule, and his father is a major landowner in that same area of France. While not conclusive, these bits of information seem consistent with my theory that Coroner de Adynton and Lord de Glissaude are conspiring to move a large number of the king's new gold coins to that part of France where, with the aid of de Glissaude's father, they plan to turn those coins to profit and escape discovery."

I calmed down as we discussed the idea and what might be done to disrupt such a theft. After considering several options, we settled on the plan of contacting the king's agent in Oxfordshire. He would have the authority to take action. It would be a feather in the cap of the king's agent and could lead to a promotion for him and possibly a manor as his reward. If our story is believed. "And if it is true," Houkyn reminded me.

"If not," I ruefully agreed, "we could be the culprits!"

Houkyn paused, glanced at me, and chuckled. "I once met the king's agent at a session of the county court but doubt that he would remember me. Perhaps we should put our information on paper and then request a meeting with him at his earliest convenience. This would protect us from appearing to overstate our case and give the king's agent something to work with. It must be carefully written, Thomas."

I agreed and offered to craft a record of our information for Houkyn's review.

Then I told him that I must meet Rebecca this afternoon but didn't mention what I had to say to her, as I was still composing the words in my head. "I will begin drafting our document tomorrow," I said, and left for the Rowley house, with the benevolent expression on his face still in my mind's eye.

* * *

The hour of nones resounded from the local bell tower. Be as they may of the canonical hours, for me the bells rang the time I had agreed to meet Rebecca at her house. So I hurried along, not wanting to miss a moment with her. I arrived a short while after she did and almost knocked at the door. Sounds from her room through curtains and a slightly open window reminded me that she might be changing out of her work clothes. I waited until the door to her room signaled that she was done and knocked upon the front door. She opened it quickly and greeted me warmly with a kiss and a long hug. Neither of us seemed inclined to end our embrace after such a long time apart, but we each had something to say to the other.

"I have received disconcerting news while you were in Reading. An agent for my still-legal master is reported to be in town, looking for me and offering a reward to anyone who will inform him of my whereabouts. I believe he has come because I am approaching my year and a day free in Oxford, and he has less than a week to take me prisoner."

"You must be terrified! But how will he be able to identify you as the runaway villein?"

"I am shocked and worried, yes. But from the day I first arrived in Oxford I have done much to hide who I am. I have adopted a new name, grown my hair very long so as to hide the marking placed on my neck by his lordship by law, and I've learned to speak everyday English in place of the French dialect spoken by the villeins on the manor, as the master will speak only French. And through no part of my own doing, I have grown six inches in height, and my breasts have become more full and pronounced. You are the only person in Oxford who knows my story and has offered to help me avoid being recaptured in the next six days. Even the girls with whom I share this house are unaware of who I really am."

"Six days is not such a long time, when we are together—during which I can help keep you hidden!"

"Do you have any ideas for me to avoid capture?"

"I do! We can move you from place to place each night. You could stay in my room at the Widow's boardinghouse one night. Then I could get Coroner Houkyn to let you stay at the coroners' meeting room one night, and on the following night you might stay at your own house. We'd start again at the Widow's, then at the meeting room, and finally back at your house. Then you would be a free woman, beyond the reach of your former master."

"Oh Thomas! You are so thoughtful and clever! I love you very much—and want to be with you forever!"

"I'm happy to hear you say you want to be with me forever. I, also, want us to be together. Will you marry me?"

"Yes, Thomas, yes. I will marry you!"

The joy I was feeling at that moment was reflected in Rebecca's eyes, which were shining through her tears. She threw her arms about my neck so very tight that for a brief moment I feared she would stop my breathing. She realized what she was doing to me and released her hold just as I began coughing and gasping for breath.

"Oh Thomas, forgive me! I was so overwhelmed that I failed to realize my own strength."

I took a couple of deep breaths, and that allowed me to recover and then to speak. "You are a strong woman! I will remember that when we enter into marriage and will never surprise—or anger you!"

We laughed and felt each other's relief in truly being together.

"Now, Thomas, now that we have expressed our desire to

marry, how do we bring it about? Can we find a priest today who will marry us?"

"I don't know all that is required for us to become husband and wife, but I am sure that we need to speak with a priest and find out. The only one I know—who ministers to the needs of my father and the residents of his manor—is Father Adam. He is some distance from here. I could travel home and ask his guidance, but you cannot leave Oxford, or the law will not free you. Do you know any priest here?"

"No, I do not."

"Then I will travel to Father's manor and seek the guidance of Father Adam, but not until you have completed your year and a day and are a free woman! It is but six days. Avoiding him while staying in Oxford must be our sole focus!"

She thought for a moment and agreed.

"This day I will seek permission from Coroner Houkyn to hide you at the coroners' meeting place tonight. Then I will ask Margaret Rowley to allow you to stay in her house on the morrow and until the following morning. If both agree to my request, I will have time to determine whether your former master has truly sent his agent to Oxford in pursuit of you. The keepers of the town's gates require a nonresident to register when he seeks to enter Oxford by listing his name, where he has come from, and his purpose for coming to the town. I will visit each of the four gateways for entering the town and request permission to review the names of recent arrivals and from where they have come. If your master's agent has come to Oxford, his name and purpose should be found in the register."

"Thank you, Thomas, for helping me to gain my freedom!"

"Our freedom, my love!" Giving Rebecca a quick kiss, I left to find Houkyn. The most likely place was the coroners' meeting room, and I headed there by the most direct route, arriving just as he was preparing to leave. I explained the situation, then asked his permission to have Rebecca stay one night in the meeting room. He saw in my face the concern which drove me to make this unusual request and quickly gave his permission. I thanked him and promised it was for just one night.

Next, I returned to the boardinghouse and found the Widow cleaning the kitchen following the morning meal. "Widow Rowley! I have a very unusual request to make. The woman whom I will soon marry is being stalked by a bounty hunter. If he is able to capture her in the next few days, the person who hired him will pay well to have her in his control. She ran away from his manor almost a year ago, and if she can avoid his agent for the next six days she will become a free woman, no longer a villein who belongs to the manor owner. I ask your permission to allow her to stay in my room tomorrow night. Then I will move her to another place the following day. I would gladly pay you whatever you ask if you agree to my request."

"You have been a good tenant, paid me promptly each week, and never caused any trouble. I agree to your request—but with two conditions. You must not engage in any inappropriate behavior with your young lady while she is in this house, and you will not pay me anything for her stay."

"I give you my word that I will honor your first condition, but I am puzzled by your second."

"As you will remember, you paid me before you went away to Reading for six days recently. You ate no meals here that you had paid for, so I will repay you by letting your young lady stay here with no charge."

"You are most generous, Widow Rowley, and I thank you for granting my request! Her name is Rebecca, and she, too, will abide by your house rules. My only request is that you not tell any of the other boarders the reason why she is here. If they ask, you could say that she is my cousin, here for a very brief visit, and she will be leaving the next day to travel to my father's manor for a visit."

"That I will do, gladly!"

With places for Rebecca secured for the next two nights, I set out for Oxford's south gate.

The chief gatekeeper was on duty when I arrived, and I

told him that I was conducting an investigation for the Oxford Coroners Office and needed to review the list of recent arrivals to see if we could identify one believed to be here seeking a young woman residing in the town. I told him that the young woman had told me she was afraid that this man intended to grab her and take her to one who would purchase her for his personal pleasures.

The gatekeeper had never received such a request, but knew Coroner Houkyn and decided I could examine the list of new arrivals. He brought me to a room adjacent to the gate, where I could look through the list of arrivals of the previous three weeks.

I worked back in time. The winter season saw fewer new arrivals than any other of the year, with some days having as few as three, but if the weather stayed temperate there were as many as twenty. I was able to go through the most recent week in a few moments and found only one male whose reason for coming was vague enough that it might be her master's agent. I kept looking further back, and came upon an entry for a man searching for his daughter, who had suddenly disappeared from their home near Faringdon, an Oxfordshire town southwest of Oxford, about two months ago. He had included a brief description of his daughter, but except for her height and age, the description did not match Rebecca. I was about to continue scanning the list when I remembered Rebecca telling me that she had done everything possible to look, act and speak differently.

I made a note of his name, Kenric Crouse, and the date. Then I returned to my review of the other men and found no other suspects.

I went to each of the other town gates with the same story and was given access to their list of recent arrivals. But at none of those gates did I find any man listing a reason for coming to Oxford that involved a missing girl or young woman. I was convinced it was Kenric Crouse, if that was his real name.

Returning to the south gate I asked the gatekeeper for more information; he was not the person with whom I had spoken earlier in the day, but he was on duty when Kenric Crouse registered, about three weeks ago and was able to give me a partial description—dark-haired, thin, furtive looks. Crouse had been standing next to set of shelves and the top of his head came just above the top shelf, which the gatekeeper knew to be five feet high because he had built the shelves only the past summer. I thanked him for remembering these details, and gave him a silver penny to reward his craftsmanship and excellent memory.

Back again at Rebecca's house, she remembered the man's name and described him with corroborating details. Though scared that she was being hunted, she was glad to know who it was. She now had some advantage over Kenric Crouse.

Now she would talk with her employer, the owner of the tavern, about the risk she was facing. She was concerned that he might dismiss her for not telling him about her escape from the manor. I escorted her to the Hawk and Hare, just in case she was accosted by Crouse along the way.

When we arrived, she sought out the tavern manager and asked if she could speak with the owner privately. I took a seat by the door while the manager went to the back room and informed him of Rebecca's request, which he agreed to without hesitation. She was a good worker, and he saw no reason not to hear her out. "Rebecca, I was surprised by your request, but happy to oblige. Tell me what is on your mind."

"Thank you, sire! I have just learned that I am being hunted by a person who works for the manor owner where my mother and I were villeins. One year ago my mother died of an illness. My father had died previously, and there was no one to protect me. The lord of the manor was known by his villeins to be lecherous and quick to take advantage of any woman or girl under his domination. I knew that as soon as my mother was buried, he would try to have his way with me. I had heard what he had done to other girls, and did not want to be ravished as they had been. I chose to run away from the manor, even though it was winter, and I would be risking my life. I took the few small coins my mother had hidden in our modest house, her shoes and her cape, and before the master could get me in his clutches I ran north from the manor lands. I was overtaken by a snowstorm shortly after I left, and while it put me at great risk, it may have saved me because the storm prevented the master's men from pursuing me. I survived by hiding under a fir tree and wrapping myself in my mother's cape. The fir kept me from being covered by snow, and the cape kept me from freezing.

"I was fortunate that the weather following the storm was fairly mild, and I was helped along the way by cotters who let me stay overnight and gave me bits of food to sustain me on my journey. I walked for nearly a week, until I found myself on a road with a number of cottages and signs that led me to know I was nearing a large town. I had the great fortune to be offered a ride on a wagon pulled by two horses. The driver asked where I was going and agreed to help me get to Oxford. He was delivering root vegetables to the market there and agreed to tell the gatekeeper that I was his granddaughter. I slept in a church and found a place to live with two young women, when you hired me to work here doing menial tasks about the tavern—for which I am ever very grateful. When you needed a girl to wait tables in the tavern, you gave me a chance—and I have tried to serve you as best I am able.

"I have lived in Oxford for nearly a year, and in a several days, when I have lived here for a year and a day, I will win my freedom from my master—as provided for under the law. But I must not be caught by my master's agent, one Kenric Crouse, before I pass my year and a day from my arrival in Oxford. I tell you all of this in the hope that you will help me avoid being taken by Kenric Crouse, back to the manor."

"Rebecca, you have been a good worker, and my customers like being served by you. I am a fool if I don't do everything I can to keep you safe from that man! Tell me how I and the folk who work here can keep you so."

"One of your customers, a young man who works for the

Oxford coroners as their clerk, has asked me to marry him, and I have agreed. He has found different places where I can stay at night, so it's harder for Crouse to find me. But I need to work and earn enough to pay my rent and other costs. Would you let me work, out of sight, here at the tavern, for the next several days? I will wash dishes, clean the kitchen work spaces, and anything else that needs doing. And once I have passed the year-and-a-day mark and become a free person, I will work one day each week without pay—to make up to you for the days I wasn't waiting on your customers."

"That is a generous offer, but you have already repaid me through the good work you have done during the past year."

Rebecca was so touched by the owner's comment that her tears flowed freely, and she threw her arms about his neck and kissed him.

"One more thing," he said with emotion. "I will ensure witnessed documentation of your first day of employment. Just in case! I suggest we use the day you entered through the gates as a starting point.

"And now please introduce me to this young man, so that I may congratulate you together!"

We were taken aback at his thoughtfulness and our oversight, thanking him profusely.

As we walked back to her house, she took my hand and squeezed it. "You are the love of my life, and I am so happy that you asked me to walk with you just a few weeks ago. Could you imagine that we would be planning our marriage so soon? If I weren't holding your hand, I would think this is a dream from which I would never want to wake."

"Neither can I fully realize that we will marry before the end of winter! You make me feel a part of a family once again, and I love you for that. But we now have a number of days, shall we safely say, during which we must keep you away from Kenric Crouse, before you become a free woman. Do not forget that this is the most important thing we must do if we are to be able to wed—seven days at least! What do you say?"

"Well, Thomas, we'll just have to hide together in safety from the cold nights, won't we!"

We walked the rest of the way to Rebecca's house in thoughtful silence. She asked me to come in, and I was glad for more time with her and to warm up before the walk to the Widow's.

"I wish I could go with you to meet your father, and to see how a manor is operated by an honorable and caring man. But more immediate is the need for you to escort me to the coroners' meeting room where I am to spend tonight. At what time should we go there?"

"I suggest, as darkness descends on Oxford, so it will be more difficult for Crouse to see you or know where you will be overnight. I have been thinking that I should stay at the meeting room with you tonight. What if he sees us as we walk there and then sees me leave without you. He would know you are there alone. He could wait until the beadles have passed by the meeting room on their hourly patrol and then try to break in to get you. Would you object to my staying there with you?"

"You have given me reason to be worried, so I would be pleased to have you with me." So it was decided that she should pack some clothes, and I would return with my knife and a half loaf of the Widow's bread.

At the boardinghouse, I told Widow Rowley that I was going to accompany Rebecca to a place in Oxford where she would stay overnight but would return here in the morning. I asked if I might take with me a half loaf of her delicious bread. She agreed, and wrapped the it in a cloth along with a container of her own churned butter. I thanked her, placed the bread and butter in my satchel, put on my winter coat and left for Rebecca's.

She was waiting for me when I knocked at the door, and bidding good night to her roommates, we headed for our destination. We walked quickly and took turns looking back to see if we were being followed. At one point she thought she saw someone who resembled Crouse behind us. We turned at the next corner and stepped into the shadows cast by a large house. After waiting five minutes, no person came around the corner, but as a precaution we continued down the street to the next corner where we turned to our destination and increased our pace. We arrived at the meeting room having seen no one else. I quickly unlocked the door; we both stepped in, and the door was locked from the inside, all in the space of one minute.

I lit a fire to ease the chill, and we arranged some chair cushions on the floor—assuming either of us could sleep with the concern we shared that Crouse might have learned where we would spend the night. We sliced some bread and slathered butter on it, then ate it while listening for any sound.

"I'll stay awake so you can sleep," I proposed, and she was tired enough that she didn't object. I listened for a few hours without hearing anything like an effort to gain entrance but struggled to stay awake. The silence was lulling me towards sleep, and by the middle of the night it had won the battle.

It must have been an hour later when a sound outside the meeting room jarred me awake. It wasn't clear what had caused the noise, and I didn't hear it again, but the anxiety kept me awake for quite some time, and I moved about the room listening for anything. I heard the wind, and once heard the call of the beadle as he passed the building while making his rounds, but I didn't hear any suspicious sounds for the rest of the night.

Rebecca woke before dawn, a bit stiff from sleeping on seat cushions but relieved that nothing had happened. "Were you able to stay awake during the night?"

"Yes I did, mostly. It seems that Crouse has not been able to find you—so far. Let us return this room to how it was when we arrived. Soon most people will be on their way to work or the market, and we can join them with less risk of being seen."

We then sliced the rest of the bread, buttered it and enjoyed breaking our fast while hearing the sounds of people passing the room; then we set about joining them. At Rebecca's house, she donned her work attire, and I accompanied her to the tavern, gave her a kiss before she went to work, promising to meet her when she was ready to leave.

I returned to the coroners' meeting room to ask Houkyn to allow me to take three days away from work in order to visit Father and to consult with the priest. He was not there, but I was told by coroner de Whatele that he was expected before midday. I stayed and talked with Coroners de Whatele and de Geddyng about the trip Houkyn and I had taken to Reading, avoiding any comment about what we had learned regarding the king's Reading mint. Houkyn arrived as we finished our conversation, and he invited me to join him for a walk.

"Sir, I have a request. I have proposed marriage to Rebecca, and she has agreed, but we do not have a priest to perform the marriage ceremony. I would like to travel to my father's manor, both to tell him of my plan to marry and to talk with the priest who serves his manor and the small village nearby about what the Church requires in order to be married. Assuming that the Church's requirements can be met, I would like him to perform the marriage ceremony. Would you allow me to take a few days? I believe I can accomplish everything necessary in three or four days, including time to travel there and back."

"I congratulate you on your impending marriage! The winter is a slow period for the coroners, so you have my approval to be away for up to five days, just in case there is a significant snowfall while you are away. When do you expect to leave?"

"Thank you, sir! I would like to travel as soon as Rebecca has completed her year and a day in Oxford and is free from the control of her diabolical master. She will pass that anniversary in a matter of days, depending who is counting, and assuming that her master's agent, Kenric Crouse, is unsuccessful in his efforts to capture and return her to her master's manor."

"Do you know that Kenric Crouse is here in Oxford?"

"Yes, I have reviewed the list of nonresidents at the gates." I told him of my discovery of the evidence and Rebecca's corroboration.

"Thomas, with your permission, I would ask the Oxford-shire sheriff, John de Alvetone, to have one of his men make inquiries for Crouse at inns hereabouts, and if he is located to warn him of the consequences of harassing residents of the town."

"You have my permission, kind sir! And I'm confident you would have Rebecca's also. Thank you for helping us prevent him from taking her away from me! I will tell her tonight. Knowing that the enforcers of the law in Oxfordshire will be looking out for any sign that he is stalking her will certainly help reduce her fear of being snatched up by him. Now I will spend the day marshalling the evidence and argument into our draft report on the double leopards, with some peace of mind."

When the time for Rebecca to finish her work at the tavern was nearing, I left the meeting room. It was my intent that she should never be out in public without me to protect her, until she had gained her freedom.

I was waiting outside the tavern's rear entrance when she emerged and greeted her with a hug and the news from Houkyn that harassing or threatening any female resident of Oxford would bring the Sheriff's men down on Crouse forthwith.

X

WHENCE THE LAW?

⋐ ⋑

R EBECCA HAD NEVER BEEN INSIDE the Rowley house and was curious to see how I had been living. She got me thinking of all that had happened to me after I walked through the gates in October. It has since been noted by friends and detractors that I was at the time sans horse, my father having declared that if I were to be such a fool, I could travel like a villein, on foot! Here I was to marry such a one. I could but chuckle.

As we walked, I told her that Sir Arthur had allowed me up to five days to travel to my family manor and to consult with Father Adam on what was required to be married.

Church services being mainly for the religious hierarchy and the well-connected, neither of us attended church in Oxford nor had we any relationship with a local priest. I had only looked in on a mass or two, out of curiosity about the impressive architecture. The priests had their backs to the curious pilgrims and folk milling around and talking over the echoing Latin. And there was nowhere to sit, so I did not stray long and left with the comings and goings. Most churches were empty of the common folk much of the time. Unless we formally joined a local church, our only option was to be married at Father's manor. She was agreeable to being married there but uncomfortable about joining a local church, wherever that may be.

With her year-and-a-day goal now six days away, as secured and witnessed in the record of her first day of employment, I asked if it would be acceptable for me to leave for father's manor thereafter, assuming no bad weather.

"I will miss you and will have an empty feeling in my heart until you return. But go and travel safely, my love!"

I wondered what I would ask of Father Adam—and how I would tell my father of our plan to marry. Would he object to my marrying beneath my station—into the family of an escaped villein? Would this be the last straw in our relationship?

She broke my thoughts by asking that we take a circuitous route to her house, where she would pick up what she needed to stay at the Widow's. We took many turns again and backtracked to be sure we were not followed and did the same when we left her house. Fortunately we still reached the Widow's in time for supper.

Rebecca had heard me speak of several of my fellow residents at the boardinghouse, but had never met any of them. She was welcomed to the dinner table, and quickly joined the conversation. I explained that she was a cousin visiting me for a day or two while in Oxfordshire and would be continuing her travel to my father's manor very soon. Out of courtesy, the diners did not directly interrogate their new guest but turned to other topics, including, to my dismay, my recent trip to Reading with the chief Oxford coroner. Once again, I lied my head off, but only briefly, to keep it on my shoulders, so to speak. The dark side of the law kept coming home to me.

But I talked about the very tasty meal the Widow had prepared and our anticipation of dessert. She didn't disappoint anyone when she went to the kitchen and returned with a pan of apple dumplings. Its appearance quickly ended the conversation as each of us fell upon our share with religious abandon.

The hour was growing late; some of the diners excused

themselves and returned to their rooms. I helped the Widow Margaret to clear the table and offered to wash the dishes. She thanked me but told me it was time for Rebecca and me to retire for the night. I accepted our dismissal graciously, and we went to my room. This was the first time that we would spend the night together, though not in the same bed. I would keep my promise to the Widow about "inappropriate behavior," but Rebecca and I cuddled and kissed until exhaustion required me to surrender the bed and sleep on the floor.

We awoke early and dressed quickly, Rebecca into her work clothes. We broke our fast with leisurely slices of the Widow's oat-bread and butter. The rising sun had yet to chase away the morning chill. We blended into the flow of people heading to their work. We felt safe from Kenric Crouse, as long as there were many around us. I left her at the Hawk and Hare, promising to return at the end of her shift.

I went to the south gate in hopes of meeting someone who was leaving the town and traveling in the direction of Father's estate. I wished to send a letter letting him know that I would be coming for a brief visit within about a week of the letter's arrival, alerting him I had important good news. Of the first six men I approached, none were going that way. But the seventh said that he would be happy to be the messenger. I gave him a shilling, and thanked him for his willingness.

Before returning to the coroners' meeting room, I decided to go looking for a seller of clothes, in hope of finding a coat that was warmer than mine, as I was likely to run into some very chilly weather on my trip home. I went directly to the shop of Alain du Ponte, where the owner bought and sold used clothing. It was where I had purchased a coat and other items for Rebecca, after she froze herself shopping for our celebration.

When I entered, I was again astounded by the variety of clothes and footwear he offered for sale. I described my journey. He studied me for a moment, and then took me to the back of his business where he had several winter coats displayed. He invited me to try them on. I did so and pointed out two of them and inquired about the price. He quoted me a price for each. I offered a lesser amount for the one. He gave me another, then lowered his price. I agreed. He accepted my several coins, thanked me, and helped me to put on my newly reused coat. I thanked him and promised again to refer others to his business.

From there I walked the short distance to the coroners' meeting room and found Houkyn. He admired my new coat and said it was a prudent investment in preparation for traveling to see my father in the midst of winter. And without further delay, he informed me that a sheriff's deputy, sent looking for Kenric Crouse at inns and other places offering overnight accommodation in Oxford, had come upon him at a small pub with an inn located just up from the south gate. He put Crouse on notice that he was being watched by the sheriff's office and was warned that threatening, intimidating or attempting to kidnap a resident of Oxford would not be tolerated. When the deputy checked at the inn later that day, he was told that Mr. Crouse had paid his bill and left town to return home.

I was still in a state of elation when Houkyn turned to our ongoing discussion and my draft report concerning the possible connection of coroner de Adynton with the theft of the king's as yet unissued double leopards. He had perused my work well by now; we needed to finalize it and decide what to do next. A mistake at this stage could be disastrous, even fatal. We avoided speaking too much about the risk, but we realized that if treason were involved with persons of great power, it could turn out to be convenient for the ax to fall on our necks—instead of any that might embarrass a king who was claiming the rule of France with his royal marks and emblems of leopards and French fleurs de lys designed in gold. Of course, the ax would be too good for the likes of us, or at least the mere son of a knight.

"We must tread like leopards on the hunt, Thomas, I am sure you agree. The connection between Lords Ricard de Adynton and de Glissaude is of course, I think, probable but not proven. In addition, our investigation in and around Reading, not to mention the manors of Sir Ricard, is arguably outside our jurisdiction."

"I understand that the pieces of theory are linked by bits of information that could be interpreted in more than one way. But when put together they ask this question: Why would a few local individuals with no discernible outside connections be such fools as to carry out such a significant theft from the king? For such a scheme to succeed, it requires people with the knowledge and capability to move gold coins that are intended to be famous, from the mint and secretly take them to places beyond the king's reach, where those double leopards can be safely sold for money that cannot be traced."

"It is a plausible theory, and your questioning about the ability of a few locals in Reading to carry out such a complicated scheme rings true to me. But theories will not convict those beyond the Reading area, who may profit from the scheme more than either the mint officials or Antoine de Glissaude himself. If we are to capture or find evidence that links those other conspirators to this brazen scheme, we will need the aid of the king's government. This brings us again to the king's representative here in Oxford. Like it or not, facts can depend on who is looking at them, eh?—"

Houkyn was right, and I realized with some trepidation that the zeal of a clerk could betray the leopard's spots to the king's representative. Though the evidence was strong, the two local participants, Edward Bellemere and Robert d'Antonio were august members of the community. But even with Lord de Glissaude, the three lacked the ability to carry out the movement of the coins to a group of people with the knowhow and contacts that could turn this from a petty crime for hanging at crossroads into a capital offense demanding greater attention. But if they could do it with the help of higher and more widespread powers, could not others do so as well? I trembled inwardly at the thought.

And what if the scheme became known, and the crown had not taken action to hunt down all the people who were participants in this crime? It would be a black mark sullying the image and the hopes of one of England's best and most successful monarchs. He would be mauled by his own leopards, while the coroner and his clerk would be left dangling, perhaps quite literally, in the wind. Henceforth, the thought of the man hanging, who greeted me at the crossroads on the way to seek my fortune in Oxford, haunted me. Had he been guilty when convicted of thievery? or just guilty of being born— The smell of death was catching up with me again.

Houkyn was right, and I told him so. "Sir, how do we get the king's agent's attention on this, in the right way?—especially with the king leading the English soldiers and with allies in France against the rival French monarch. He would be unable to return to England to hear us out. We need someone in the king's government to lend a sympathetic ear to our evidence and reasoning. One with the authority to initiate an investigation at the highest level, to follow the crime up the chain to those who would profit the most at the king's expense and embarrassment!"

"Let us review once more the written report—as if our very lives depend on it, shall we, Thomas?" the coroner said with a less-than-reassuring smile.

It was clear that finding a high-ranking person with the requisite authority was no small feat, and Houkyn did not wish to pick someone only to be rejected in his plea for investigating those who could be the higher-ups in the crime. This could be the fatal mistake, especially if the official he chose to hear us out not only knew some of the likely leaders but was a conspirator himself. The revolving thought of this possibility caused my belly to tighten again and again and the sweat to flow profusely from my brow. Neither of us wanted to speak about it, but we did.

"Yes, sir, the report is key to success, indeed, and there must be copies. If the person we approach happens to know one or more of the leaders of this scheme, or worse yet—"

"Yes, yes, the situation is quite clear enough to us both. Shall we get to work?"

Once we decided we had finalized the coroner's special report, Houkyn proceeded to list the names of the king's top administrators, long-time allies, whom he thought least likely to risk such an underhanded scheme for money alone. "As to the motive of discrediting the monarch, Thomas, I must confide that I am rather at sea politically these days, or should I say 'at war—endless war!' " and he chuckled ruefully. So many enemies of the monarchy and who knows how many spies. I cannot possibly be privy to any of that, so we will have to take a risk. Are you with me?"

I did not hesitate to say yes to this honest fellow, though I knew it might be the single most important word of my life.

"Good, Thomas! Good man! So the name that comes to my mind is that of William Edington, formerly Edward III's keeper of the wardrobe, and recently appointed by the king to be the treasurer of the realm. He is also a bishop of highest respect. By his close personal service to king and realm, he seems the person who can best be trusted with our information, and most able to initiate investigation of this crime against king and country. He is in London, unlike the king and his military officers. I will make inquiries of the king's man based in Oxford, to see how to arrange a meeting with Edington, at his earliest convenience, regarding evidence of a scheme to steal items of great personal value to the king during his absence. I only hope our local agent of the crown will see sense in withholding the report and thereby protecting anyone else from getting compromised between great powers of the realm."

Houkyn put on his coat. "Wish me luck, Thomas!"

"Us both!" And he was off to find the king's direct representative in Oxford. The coins on which the king was placing so much importance could gain the kind of impact and respect for England that the gold florin had for the City of Florence in achieving leadership in money and banking on the mainland. The thought shuddered through my soul.

* * *

Daniel Latimer was the king's agent in Oxford. The visit from the chief coroner, tipping him off with due gravitas as to an unspeakable treachery, was enough to set in motion the delivery of an encoded message from Latimer to his superior in the king's government. Marked as Top Secret, it was sent by fast courier early the next morning. Traveling by the most direct route to London and changing horses every ten miles, the courier reached the city before the winter sun slipped away that same day. It had helped things along that the coroner had shown Latimer a single double leopard as evidence.

The further result was a return visit from David Latimer, who informed Houkyn that Bishop William Edington, treasurer of the realm, would be arriving in Oxford in two days, traveling incognito. He would be accompanied by the head of the King's Palace Guard and a security detail.

Houkyn and I were directed to say nothing about the visit, its purpose, who was coming, or anything else related to this matter. Latimer would arrange for a private place where Edington and the captain of the Palace Guard could meet with the chief coroner and his clerk. Latimer would take us to that location once our visitors had arrived. In a world where decisions are made over weeks and actions taken over months, this quick and seemingly positive response was heartening. Even so, Houkyn and I privately evinced some disquiet at being sequestered in close quarters with a commanding knight of the Palace Guard.

In the next two days, I made copies of the full report on which our lives might depend, and we secured them in different locations.

Agent Latimer arrived with a soldier of Bishop Edington's security. They were timely and quickly escorted us to a small room in the Oxford Courts building. We laid out our materials and the written statement outlining how we had come to this point in our investigation. When we told him we were ready, he left the meeting room and returned with the bishop. We quietly breathed a sigh of relief when the security was excused to stand guard outside the building.

We had assumed that the holder of such an important position in the king's government and the hierarchy of the Church would arrive dressed in a fashion befitting his office, but we were surprised when Edington walked in dressed in his riding clothes, still dusty from the road and certainly incognito. That sight eased my mind about the type of person we were about to meet and who might hold the scales of justice with us in them.

He was here because he recognized that we had potentially uncovered a matter of such importance that immediacy won out over formality. His first words reinforced that message. "Gentlemen, if what you relayed to me through Agent Latimer proves to be half as important as it appears, it would still be the most outrageous act of treason against the king and realm ever to come to my attention as treasurer. On behalf of the king, I thank you for your efforts in bringing this matter to our attention and for providing a picture of how the thefts were being achieved without discovery—before you came upon the purse of the ten double leopards.

"I understand from Agent Latimer that you have prepared a text laying out precisely your investigation, the evidence you have collected, and your theory on why this is much more than a local theft of opportunity.

"I would like to review your text first and then ask you some questions. My security person has taken the liberty of bringing some food and beverage for you to enjoy, while I study your document. Please accept this as a small token of our debt to you."

We thanked him for his consideration and the well-chosen fare being set at a table to one side of the room. It was most flavorful and of honest local produce. But we were especially interested, without wishing to appear obtrusive, in the thorough way in which he scrutinized our information and made notes regarding some of the items. This appeared to be a serious man intent on understanding a scheme that was audacious and so subtle that it had been discovered only by way of the unsolved death of an unknown man at the hands of an as-yet-unproven perpetrator—with a pouch of coins tossed aside, found by the thorough techniques of the coroner. Refreshed at the sideboard, I began to feel that the schemers were about to meet more than their match at the hands of Bishop Edington and the monarchy.

When Houkyn and I were called and formally introduced to Sir Daniel Gantry, captain of the guard at the table where they had been poring over the documentation with Agent Latimer, we felt even more at ease. The bishop asked the coroner to recount the whole story and the clerk to fill in the parts where he alone was present, such as the tracking of d'Antonio and the conversation with Alfred at the boardinghouse, or if I might have anything to add to what Houkyn was saying. As we spoke our parts, the bishop partook of some leftovers from the sideboard, choice pieces we had been careful to leave alone.

He was particularly interested in the clever way that Bellemere had apparently staged the counting and recounting of the double leopards kept in the secured mint boxes. He called it a sleight of hand done to make us think it was a good count because different counters had counted each box the second time. He felt that a surprise raid on the mint by the king's officers and the seizing of the manager's private files would probably show two sets of records. He appreciated Houkyn's insistence that the manager and assistant prepare a list of any local persons who had been given a tour of the mint. He believed that Bellemere and d'Antonio had prepared a list with several local names in hopes of throwing suspicion onto innocent men, such as Spencer, away from Antoine de Glissaude, the likely suspect.

Houkyn credited me for suspecting a departure from the mint. He noted that had I not kept watch from nearby and observed d'Antonio slipping out onto the path to Longate manor, we would have missed a key piece of information.

I confess that I blushed. Bishop Edington laughed good-heartedly and put his hand on my shoulder with gratitude. He also enjoyed the schemes the coroner and the bailiff had created for John the villein in his courageous return to face his vicious master and as the key witness against the fictitious Orvyn Barber. The bishop commented that it sounded like Italian theater. I hoped this was a good thing.

He questioned me further about the four major traders who live in or near Oxford and any other information I had elicited from Alfred Rowley about those men and their primary trading routes. Then he turned to Houkyn for any corroboration from a long experience in Oxford.

He commended me for recognizing that Ricard de Adynton's largest manor was in Buckinghamshire, just across the shire border from Reading, as was Longate Manor. He was aware that de Glissaude came from a part of France under English control, with family yet living in that part of the country. He reflected aloud that if a strong link could be made between de Adynton and de Glissaude, it would lead to their arrest. "No doubt they would endure the tender mercies of His Majesty's dungeon machines to discover their co-conspirators. Though I imagine that under those conditions I should myself say anything at all—unless I were to suffer the fate of the martyrs, of course, I hope." To which there was a solemn moment when I could not erase the hanged man from the crossroads of my memory.

Finally, after several hours of intense discussion, Bishop Edington stood and said, "My friends and loyal supporters of King Edward III, you have persuaded me that you have provided critically important evidence that has exposed this treason to the light of day. Your efforts will be well rewarded, I am sure, both in the near future and also when the king is able to return from France following victory in the war."

Little did I know the war would still persist, even now as I write in the final chapter of a long, long life.

Be that as it may, Bishop Edington continued, "I will personally tell the king of your dedication, cleverness, and insightfulness in discovering this crime and identifying the key local offenders. I ask that you not speak of any of this to anyone other than each other until the king's government can bring its investigators to follow the leads you have identified and locate all other parties involved in this scheme. Once we are able to round up them all and put them on trial, I will urge the king, in the strongest terms, to reward you both in ways worthy of the work you have done and the risks you have taken for justice. Do not be surprised if our investigators ask for your further assistance, as they try to piece together additional information."

There was an awkward pause, while the air hung about me.

"So, I will be returning to London tomorrow!" He recovered his conviviality, "But I request that you join me for dinner this evening in my quarters. I wish to know more about both of you, as I would like to be able to assist your advancement in the future, myself!"

After Bishop Edington returned to his rooms in the Oxford Courts building, Houkyn suggested we take a walk.

I didn't know how he was reacting to Edington's final words, but for me they opened my mind to where I might want to go in my future life. We had quickly accepted his invitation. But my mind was already turning to the implications of having the treasurer of the realm and closest person to the king after his son, the Black Prince, offer to assist in my advancement. Did I want to become a lawyer? Have my own manor with land sufficient to support its operation? Study at Oxford University? Travel the country and abroad? Write of the history of England? The ideas poured out in a flood, as if a dam long holding back my future had suddenly been breached, overwhelming what I had thought already to be great good fortune to date.

I think Sir Thomas, too, was wondering what the assistance Edington could offer. While he was at least twenty-five years my senior, he could still have things he would wish to do—or be—in his remaining life. In the several months I had worked for Houkyn, he had never spoken of his private life. I knew he was a knight and freeholder; coroners were selected from these groups within the district. But I knew little more beyond the fact that he was married and had three children. The conversation during our walk would likely be revealing.

The weather that day was more temperate than usual for the winter, the sun was not obscured by the clouds, and there was little breeze, making conditions conducive to a leisurely stroll about the area around the Oxford Courts building. Dinner would be in about two hours, so we had time to walk and talk at length. Houkyn began our conversation by expressing his gratification with Edington's willingness to assist in our advancement. He asked if I had given thought to any such help Edington might provide me.

"Yes, his offer stunned me at first, but my mind quickly grasped the implications, and ideas came flooding into my head, bumping into one another, and giving me such a sense of possibility for choosing my future path, rather than letting life point my way."

I mentioned things which had already entered my mind. The possibilities were so many that I was sure I could not tell him that night what I would want the most, as it could change by morning. I hoped Edington would allow us time to reflect on how he might assist us and not press for an answer. "What have you considered since hearing those words that could open many doors?" I asked.

Houkyn, already settled into his life, spoke of smaller things a bishop and treasurer might offer. As he talked, I sensed that he was somewhat disappointed in his less-than-positive status within the group of knights and wealthy freeholders in Oxford, who were his peers. True, they had elected him at the town court to be the lead coroner, but he felt as if they had done so because they did not want the position with all the work required. His price for acceptance among them was to do what they wished not to do. And he seldom had the opportunity to meet and talk with his electors, except when death or crime necessitated that they converse. He wanted Edington to help him achieve a better status within this group of equals, where they would seek him out, and not the reverse.

He had other thoughts. To have a manor with sufficient fertile land and water to make it more profitable than his own.

He revealed that his ancestors had begun the process of saving money and slowly acquiring small parcels of land, first for their own use and later to be leased out to other peasants for modest rents. In time, they had accumulated enough land and rents collected to become part of the merchant class, buying and selling goods, offering services, and later lending small amounts of money to others pursuing a better future, as they had. It was based on this steady climb to be a freeholder—and eventually a knight—that had brought Sir Arthur Houkyn to his present position.

We alluded to the bishop's power over lands taken from lords who had opposed the king—a power to grant a portion to either or both of us. He could no doubt grant us rights to some type of asset or resource that would yield a regular stream of revenue. It was possible for him to request that the king appoint either of us to a position with a handsome income. My mind was afire, and I feared it might be a sin.

We mulled in confidence the question of Bishop Edington's offer of "advancement" as regards the law. Where was equity? Were we to benefit from a just war against the French? A war for lands held by Frenchmen? What if Lady Justice was on the side of those who had lost their lands in opposition to the king here and abroad, a king who was therefore but a common thief and evermore deeply in debt t'boot—and desperate for the organizational and accounting expertise of his bishop-treasurer? Was there another side of the coin in the valor of the treasonous thieves?

Having thoroughly frightened and exhausted ourselves with ethics and natural law, the conversation lagged, and we came back to the here and now and the need to rally ourselves convincingly. A shifty countenance on either of us could invite the ecclesiastical glare of suspicion and we'd be done for.

The prospect of a tasty repast provided the needed focus for me. Was there any small request we might make at dinner, or would that risk losing the opportunity of gaining something more in the not-too-distant future?

There was one such that came to my mind suddenly, which
would meet a need I had so far been unable to resolve. I would
ask him, a bishop, to marry Rebecca and me—tomorrow
morning, before he leaves for London!

The hour for our dinner was quickly approaching, so we
turned back towards the Courts building and entered just as
a local food preparer and his assistant were bringing in the
elements of our dinner. This was not to be a fancy affair, just a
delicious meal with a variety of dishes to try. We stepped back
to watch the men lay out at least five courses, each covered to
hold in the heat, along with a special bottle of wine chosen to
go with each course. My mouth began to water.

Moments later Edington descended from his rooms and
joined us. First he poured each of us a glass of a chilled white
wine that had an aroma of spring fruits, and then he toasted us
for our service to the king. We replied with humble gratitude.

Then he confided, "I know that if King Edward were here
with us, he would thank you personally for all that you have
done to stop the theft of the golden double-leopard coins,
coins he had designed to mark England's emergence as a major
center of trade and culture and a competitor with Florence and
their gold florins. They are to be released upon his return from a
victorious war in France, and I am certain that he will want both
of you to be present at the ceremony, to be honored for your
work unearthing the scheme hatched involving the Reading
mint." We quaffed in appreciation.

"It goes without saying," he added reflectively, twirling
slightly his wineglass, "that henceforth the minting of double
leopards will be at the Tower of London. They may already
have presses in place there, what?" We all chuckled, some more
than others. I felt judged. But surely that was a natural reaction.

A faint atmosphere of honor among thieves brought
increasing levity, until the bishop remarked, "I have told you
of my wish and intent to assist you in advancing in the world.
Tonight I want to learn more about each of you, and where you
might wish to have your future lives go. It is unlikely that I can

grant any aspiration this night, but what I learn about you will enable me to watch for and create opportunities that can enable you to achieve the life you wish to live. But let us begin with grace and then to dine on this fine meal!"

As we saw fit and timely, Houkyn and I spoke of the many ideas which have entered our thoughts since hearing his words earlier in the day about his offer of assistance. When it came my chance, I spoke first of getting an education beyond my ten years at Ravley Abbey, knowing from my time studying with Brother Kenric and the monks at the abbey that an educated mind opens many doors.

He nodded at my placing education at the top of my list; then he asked what type of education I might wish to pursue. In response, I said one that taught me how to learn, because once I knew how to learn, I could always learn what I needed or wished. He looked at me with a broad grin upon his face and noted that what I had just said was the heart of education, and that I was well on the way to achieving my wish.

I then brought up my wish to someday soon have my own manor, with sufficient fertile land and water to make it profitable, as good land would always support me in whatever else I might do.

Lastly, I hoped to do some of my learning through travel, both here in England and on the mainland, as this would allow me to understand the differences that bring countries into war or other disputes.

"Thomas, you have just demonstrated the kind of mind and way of thinking that is desperately needed in England. You may never need my assistance, but I wish to know you for the remaining years of my life, because you have achieved a level of wisdom from which I might learn. I pray that we will always be friends! Is there anything else you wish to say?"

Yes sire! Would you do the honor of performing my marriage to my beloved Rebecca, who tomorrow will pass one year and a day living in Oxford and thus becoming a free person, released from her villein status from a manor she left following her mother's death. We met just a few months ago, but our love has grown to the point where we wish to marry. Unfortunately, neither of us have a priest we can ask to perform the service. Would you do the honor of making us husband and wife? It need not be now, but we would like to be married by the coming spring. If you would do this, we would travel to wherever you are in order to be wed."

The bishop leaned back in his chair and allowed himself an Old Testament fragment from Proverbs, "Whoever oppresses a poor man insults his Maker—

"Thomas, 'tis I would be honored. While I must return to London on the morrow to meet with others in the king's government, I would be glad to return to Oxford to marry you together within a month. This would allow you time to invite your family, friends and colleagues and to plan a celebration of your marriage. Would that be an acceptable answer, my friend?"

"Yes, my lord bishop, that would make Rebecca and me very happy, and my father as well!— I did not elaborate.

"Pray let us know what day would be convenient for you in the next month, and we will meet you at the church door that day!"

"Consider it my wedding gift to you and Rebecca! Might you arrange for me to meet her tomorrow before I depart?"

"Yes, we will be here by three hours past prime, at the bells of terce, if that suits your schedule."

"It suits my schedule very well. I will see you then!"

The bishop thereafter entertained us with a hilarious and bawdy tale he had heard from a pilgrim about a married couple on their way to Canterbury Cathedral to visit the shrine of Thomas Becket.

But eventually His Excellency turned to Sir Arthur and heard what assistance might well be appreciated. Houkyn told him of his wish to become a more welcome member of the knights and freedmen of the town and to gain more and better land near his small manor in order to provide for his growing family. Beyond those goals, Houkyn told him that if an opportunity were to arise for filling a royal position of responsibility in Oxfordshire, he would be most interested in being considered.

"Sir, I will see what I can do to assist you in achieving your first two goals and will ask the king's chamberlain, who keeps the list of royal positions to be appointed, to let me know whenever a position in Oxfordshire requires an appointment. When one is needed, I will strongly urge the king to appoint you. And will remind him of your great service to him in a desperate time!"

Our dinner was finished, and both Houkyn and I bid our host and new friend, Treasurer of the Realm Bishop William Edington, a warm and hearty thank you and safe journey on the morrow.

"Not until I have met your Rebecca!" he replied with a twinkle in his eye I found difficult to interpret. Regardless, it would be the sixth day, and she would be a free—if not freeborn—Englishwoman.

As we walked away from the Oxford Courts building, Houkyn congratulated me again on my impending marriage and noted that Edington seemed serious in his pledge to assist us in advancing our lives. "Thomas, I do believe you have provided our lord bishop an excellent opportunity to show his saintly devotion and set an example in the marriage of a villein and the son of a knight. With a dash of politics, what!" Then he muttered under his breath, "Given those who finance the war with their taxes."

The man hanged at the crossroads was now but a ghost.

XI

TREASURES OF THE HEART

଼ ଼

I T WAS THE EVENING OF the last day of her legal enslavement.
Rebecca and I were together to celebrate. She prepared a
hearty chicken dinner with items I had purchased earlier in the
day at the winter market—turnips, onions, garlic and carrots,
along with late-season apples and a small block of cheese. I'd
also found a bouquet of parsley and herbs. As we sat down to
table, we talked about our wedding.

Earlier in the day, Bishop Edington, on meeting Rebecca,
had committed to return within a month to perform our
wedding service. He would arrive on the third Friday of
March, and depart the following Monday morning to return
to London. He suggested that I reserve the banquet room at
one of Oxford's better inns, as he intended to host a wedding
feast for us following the marriage ceremony. He included a
promissory note payable to the inn, an amount sufficient to
cover all expenses of the banquet, and directed me to deliver it
promptly to reserve the banquet room.

"What a wonderful man Bishop Edington has proved to be!"
Rebecca said. "You and Sir Arthur Houkyn are so fortunate that
he responded to your request so quickly and followed through

immediately. Your service to the king seems to have created a lasting friendship."

"If so, I believe that if our fates were ever in the balance, you won him over today." I did not wish to frighten her, and she took the compliment with grace. We raised a glass of good hard cider and dug into our feast.

* * *

Ours was no longer to be a "next-day wedding," so to speak. The lord bishop had wisely given us plenty of lead time, what with winter still bearing down upon us. We began to send invitations to those we most wanted to be with us on our wedding day—my father, Rebecca's housemates, the Widow Rowley and Alfred, Maurin Barrett, the Oxford coroners, Oxfordshire sheriff John de Alvetone, Bailiff Mallory of Reading, the owner of the Hawk and Hare Tavern, along with the cook and witnesses to the arrival document, who were also close friends, Brother Kenric. The list kept growing. We received responses in due course, including from my father, who had been expecting me at the Manor daily.

Naturally, he had been expecting a full account of the family background of the lady I was to wed, having already so well established myself in Oxford. I had prepared myself with a short speech to soften the blow over mulled wine, in comfort before the fire of the estate house library. I would recall the days of my childhood playing with the children of the villeins and go from there. The marriage being blessed by the king's close friend and financial confidant, a bishop, would take us a goodly ways and ought to smooth over any reasons for my having arrived in Oxford without a horse.

But there was little need to make the journey now that we had someone to marry us—one whose status was so elevated that, on the downside, my father's expectations had soared in receipt of the information to this effect contained in the invitation. Not that I worried. Except that I could not avoid the looming image of my father meeting the bride and entering a state of shock, the bishop notwithstanding. Though a bishop and treasurer of the realm was perhaps above pressures of close family status bearing on a humble knight, no so my father.

I could see that Rebecca was beginning to worry as well. I quipped that the king himself is not above family matters, to say the least, being at war!

This made her laugh, and we decided that I should make plain where she was from in a well-crafted letter as soon as possible and inspire him with the truth of love, defended by knights who had fought for justice and the honor of their beloved. To conjure courtly romance rung a bit hollow, and we could not help appending a series of bawdy repartee that descended into fondling and spooning.

In the main, I would simply write of her meeting with Lord Bishop Edington in glowing terms. And Father would of course understand that to withhold his blessing would be to challenge the authority and judgment of His Excellency, not to overly mention the king. I felt a guilty pleasure in this. The more we thought about how everything hung on the favor of this man of Church and Chancery, the more Rebecca's brief and simple part seemed to be the key to good fortune, pending the day of the wedding.

* * *

Our talk turned increasingly to where we might live after our wedding. My room at the Widow's was barely large enough for me. We began seeking a small house, and had the assistance of the owner of the Hawk and Hare, who lived in only one of his two houses. He asked if we might be interested in renting the other, and we went with him to see if it met our needs.

Only a half mile from the Widow's, it had five rooms and contained several items of furnishings that would be necessary, as neither of us owned a stick. Set in a small neighborhood, it had a good-size flower garden, though snow covered it for the moment, and a well of clear, cold water. It was solidly built, and the rent was reasonable, especially after the tavern owner gave Rebecca a raise in pay. With that, and some money I had been saving for a special occasion, we agreed to rent it on a year-to-year basis.

Now with a place to live, Rebecca undertook to find other items of furniture, kitchenware, and a bed with a good mattress of fresh straw. Where she found time to take care of all these important details, I could not determine, but find the time she did, asking my assistance only as needed. She was a woman possessed as she pursued the remaining items needed to make our home ready and welcoming. Where she found the bed with a new straw mattress I could only speculate, until I found that it had belonged to one of her regular customers at the tavern. He was a local merchant who bought, sold and traded a variety of household goods, and he had just made a sizable purchase of furnishings from a house about to be torn down to make room for an expansion of the Shambles, to accommodate several new butchers and cattle brokers. When he learned that Rebecca was soon to be married, he took her aside the following day at the tavern and offered it as his gift to her for her marriage bed. She was so surprised and touched by his generosity, she said she threw her arms about him and "squeezed him hard," to which I could relate!

The days passed like leaves on a stiff breeze, and then it was the week when we would be wed. I had planned to find something special to give her on our day, but had been caught up in preparing one of the coroners for an Oxford Court session, where he was to explain the conflicting evidence in a death, where it was unclear whether it was misadventure or murder. Finally, on the day before our wedding, I was able to find a silver locket on offer by a local jeweler and bought it. For an additional shilling, the jeweler agreed to engrave the words, "I will love you forever" inside the locket and to have it ready the next morning.

And then it was our wedding day! Surrounded by family,

friends and colleagues, we stood before Bishop Edington and spoke the words that made us husband and wife. He blessed our union, then invited all to join us for a wedding feast. And it was a feast like no other I had ever experienced—before or after. There must have been at least ten toasts offered—to the bride, to the groom, to the marriage, to family and friends, to Bishop Edington and, towards the end of the celebration, to the health of King Edward III in France.

As our guests departed, His Excellency took Rebecca and me aside and gave us a small box of sandalwood. Saying we should not open it until we were alone in our new home and not to tell anyone where we had got the gift—at least, not until the double leopards were well in circulation—he kissed Rebecca and placed his arm over my shoulder. "I am so happy for you and know you will be happy with one another! Be assured that I will be in touch with you henceforth and will do all I can to help you have lives that are full and fruitful." Then he turned to the door and was gone into the darkness.

I slipped the sandalwood box into my pocket, and Rebecca and I went to bid my father a goodnight, with a promise that we would break our fast with him the next morning. As he had just arrived the night before, we had hardly spoken, apart from a formal introduction to his daughter-in-law-to-be, at which he was the soul of chivalry.

Father was clearly impressed by Bishop Edington's all-encompassing bonhomie, where the guests were from many walks of life. Perhaps this was the hope and vision of the lord treasurer for a new peace under the House of Plantagenet, after years of costly warfare, with Edward himself in expensive vassalage to the king of France.

Little did we know that the wars would continue, even as I write and look to last a hundred years or more. But His Excellency made a special point personally and in a toast to my father to commend his heroism in battle and in saving the life of Edward III.

We walked to our new home, talking quietly about our hopes

for this new life together. At our door, I kissed her and we went through it together. Once inside, I brought out my gift to her and placed it around her neck. She opened the locket, saw the words engraved within, and buried her face in my neck, whispering, "I love you so much!"

XII

RINGS AND DREAMS

ભ ৪

THE AFTERNOON WAS MORE THAN half gone when I reached home, having stopped at the winter farmers market to find something for the larder. The variety of items available had been slowly declining, but I had some luck when I came upon a bag of winter apples, still firm after several months. Rebecca returned from work and began making a cobbler for the evening's dinner. While cutting up the apples, we heard a knock at the door; it was a courier from London with a fancy envelope with gold lettering, heavy with several pages of stationary. I opened it quickly, anticipating that it was from Lord Edington.

Within the first three sentences I was stunned by what I saw on the page. He had written that the king's investigators had followed through on the work that Houkyn and I had done. They now knew the three major culprits in the thefts. Two were now in custody: Lord de Glissaude of Longate Manor and Oxford coroner and trader, Lord Ricard de Adynton; the third was being hunted by the king's investigators. The lord bishop wrote that the king was now aware of the important work Houkyn and I had done. His spies had yet to determining exactly how the culprits were able to cover up their theft by falsifying the mint's records and what was their local organization. But they had set a trap and caught the major actors in international transactions, red-handed. The king had authorized his bishop to offer to both Houkyn and me, each, a manor that the king had repossessed from those disloyal to the realm. The king had also written to Bishop Edington to say that upon his return to England, following the war in France, it is his intent to make additional gifts to each of us."

The words on the page and the implications of "additional gifts" from the king were beyond comprehension, and we found it hard to appreciate the magnitude of what His Excellency had written.

We placed the letter with the sandalwood box. In the box we had found a gold double leopard on a gold chain. The haunting thought had long remained that we were sworn to secrecy over a gift that could—if matters had gone the other way and the great powers had lost out to their enemies in the misfortunes of war—could, I dare say, have incriminated us! Well, this letter put all that largely to rest. And the war did grind on with almost reassuring ambivalence. What more could one wish for of the king's favor but a manor? Beyond that, might one not be asking for trouble, if only from one's weakness?

We locked the letter and the box in one of the sturdy pieces of furniture Rebecca had bought for our new life together in a better world, where logic and evidence would reign supreme. No doubt the lord treasurer understood full well the significance of the gift and gave it with the gift of wisdom in a treacherous world. He had planned his letter well aforehand, with confidence in the capture of the traitors. And if things had not gone well, we would have a piece of gold to melt down if need be. Rebecca and I agreed not to talk about all this, except in close confidence. Especially the king's "additional gifts"—to be conferred on his return from the long wars. It was a changing world, wherein justice was in the balance as a matter of factual analysis and brute force and authority. In any case, it would not do for Rebecca to show off an emblem that might challenge a straggler who had escaped capture.

She sagely added to my theorizing. "We will keep this quiet, at least until we fully understand and appreciate the king's gift. We should not flaunt his reward to you, as there will be some who would see it as taking from one Englishman to give to another—and might wish to see it taken from you and given to them!"

"And so, my love, the good bishop has not only married us but alerted us with this gift that we are to be thrust into politics at the highest levels—not to dwell, by God!"

What we also did not dwell upon was the expectation that the king would have at least some of the conspirators hung, drawn and quartered, and their body parts displayed about the kingdom. I privately hoped there would be no further body parts at crossroads and winced at the thought of having to go out any of the gates in the near future.

Instead, she remarked that with de Adynton in prison, his position would need to be filled through an election by lords, knights and freemen of the coroners' district. She believed I now met the qualifications to be a coroner, and I replied that Houkyn had already urged the other coroners to join him in proposing me to fill the vacancy.

* * *

The following days brought weather that reminded us all that summer would be coming in soon, but before it arrived there was indeed the matter of an election to fill the vacancy left by Lord Ricard de Adynton's arrest. The gathering of the lords, knights and freeholders took place at the Oxford Courts building, where the sheriff would preside, announce the results, and certify them to the king's government. The warming weather and pleasant breezes brought out a good representation of those men of sufficient wealth and standing to qualify as voters. In total, more than one hundred were eligible and present for the vote.

It became clear that Houkyn had done a very good job of praising me as a most worthy replacement as a coroner, and there was little said by the gathering. No electioneering was allowed, and the sheriff read out both my name and that of another candidate. He then called for a show of hands in my favor, which produced overwhelming support, followed by a show of hands for the other candidate. His result was minimal, and the sheriff declared Thomas Votary to be elected as Oxford's new coroner. My fame in the town as rightful successor did no harm in securing me the position, even over a wealthy competitor. There was a good round of applause, and I thanked all who had voted for granting me this opportunity to serve Oxford.

As I walked home following my election, I met several people who had already heard the news, and some even thanked me for taking on a difficult job with no compensation. This would be a bit of a problem, as at the current time I had no regular source of income and would have to depend on funds my father could spare, until such time as I was able to take possession of the manor granted me by the king, through the treasurer of the realm. This sobering line of thought took away some of the excitement of my election and forced me to think about how I could obtain sufficient funds to support Rebecca and our house until the manor house and lands became mine and could support us. In reality, I had just lost the job I had been so excited to get a short time ago.

When I arrived at home, I was surprised to find Rebecca, many of our friends, and two of my now fellow coroners, Houkyn and de Whatele, waiting to greet me and celebrate my elevation. A cheer went up as I walked into the front yard, and Rebecca came running to give me a big kiss and a warm hug. I was overwhelmed to feel her love—and the support of our many friends, and there were tears in my eyes as I expressed my deep appreciation.

There were food and beverages aplenty, and I walked with Rebecca among our friends, exchanging stories and jests.

The celebration gradually dwindled down, as our guests

returned to work, home, business, or to complete their day. When the last took their leave, Rebecca and I sat on our front steps and talked of how fortunate we were to have such friends. As we relaxed, she leaned over and whispered in my ear—and my heart jumped a few beats from what I heard. Her few words were, "I am with child."

She said her menses had not come when expected last week, and she had a feeling in her womb since then that her mother had described to her months before she died—the feeling that she was pregnant. "Let us not speak of this to anyone until I am sure, but I think we will know within the next month. I am so happy and that you share my joy. If I am right, I would like to name the baby after your late mother if it is a girl and after my late father if a boy. Would you agree?"

"Yes my love, that is a thoughtful choice—either way! Let us go into our house and spend a quiet evening being close together treasuring this news and thinking about our future." And we did just that, talking until late about how our lives will grow together with one or more children, a manor of our own providing the resources that would enable us to live without financial worries. And we fell asleep side by side and dreamed dreams.

We awoke early, ate some of the foods left from yesterday's celebration, before I went to the meeting room and she to the Hawk and Hare.

When I arrived at the room for my first day as an Oxford coroner, de Whatele was already there. Houkyn was expected, but de Whatele was anxious to tell me what he had learned on a trip to the Northgate hundred, regarding two individuals by the name of Parr and Tanner. He was about to launch into his news when Houkyn walked in and joined us.

De Whatele described at great length a circumstance where these two lived at large and seldom returned to a manor in the hundred that they had recently visited. This probably was to reduce the risk of manor residents seeing them around so often as to arouse curiosity or suspicion. Strangers passing through the hundred were ignored for the most part, but both Parr and Tanner worked hard to keep a low profile.

One of the businesses in the hundred was a sawmill with a waterwheel, and when there was a need for extra mill workers to handle a large job, the owner would put out the word that any able-bodied man strong and skilled enough to handle the saw-logs or operate the equipment would be hired to help. Tanner often hired onto these jobs, earning extra money and meeting workers who might be interested in doing similar work—to the east. He would pass along their names and residences to Parr, who would visit in the areas near where they lived, either at home or on manorial lands, to follow up on the leads from Tanner.

After hearing him out, Houkyn observed that the two were clever in their approach to possible recruits, seeking out only those who had shown an initial interest in possibly going east for more money—and for some, an opportunity to shed their manorial obligations to their lord. Villeins might seek freedom. "You've been thorough, it seems to me, so far!" And he smiled engagingly, implying the well-known complexities of a coroner's work.

"I believe you've described the pattern of how worker recruiters operate with minimal risk. Should we let the manorial lords and people with businesses in the hundreds using workers with special talents or skills know what to be looking out for?—so they can run off the recruiters or warn their workers to steer clear?"

"I wonder," de Whatele pursued, "if there is a way to alert coroners and sheriffs in other areas closer to where these jobs are supposed to be available—of such recruiters and how they operate in spiriting valuable workers away and taking them to jobs nearer London.

"Perhaps we could invite businessmen and lords of manors in the hundred to hear what we've learned, so they can be on guard for such operators coming into their workplaces and places where their workers drink their ale."

Houkyn replied, saying that the only way to do that would be by sending communications to each shire's sheriff and chief coroner and to mayors of incorporated towns and their coroners, describing what we have seen and learned of efforts by lords of manors and freemen just west of London's suburbs to recruit, away from landowners and others further to the west. "We can safely assume, I think, that the employers are contracting, at least indirectly, with said Tanner and Parr, among others, to their mutual benefit. Skilled workers doing critical jobs are increasingly in short supply."

"So which lords of which manors and which owners of sawmills would want to hear of this?" I questioned, following up on Houkyn's implication about stirring things up.

De Whatele raised the idea that Parliament ought to be made aware of this scheme and of such organized rings, so it could debate the issue and determine whether such behavior should be prohibited to all.

But Houkyn thought that by the time Parliament had made up its mind, there would be no skilled workers left west of London's suburbs—bar an escalation of wages, accompanied by the upset of the entire social order. He gave me a wry smile.

Lord de Whatele, always up for a good political discussion, defended the status quo, what with rising crime and unsolved murders.

As I listened, I began to chuckle until they stopped talking to see why. I apologized for interrupting them but said I couldn't help thinking about how damnably difficult it would be for us to accomplish these large undertakings by ourselves. "Maybe we should form a counter-clique!"

"We'll begin with finding a new clerk," Houkyn observed merrily.

With that, I suggested an ale at the Hawk and Hare might put this all in perspective; I would buy the first round. The suggestion was well met, and out the door we went.

* * *

I walked slowly towards home, enjoying the growing warmth of the sun and the blooming of early flowers in protected spots along the street. I realized that if Rebecca has a successful pregnancy, she would give birth in the winter. We will need to purchase enough firewood this summer to carry us through the whole winter, as additional amounts needed in January will be very costly. Another expense! I would ask Alfred where we should buy the wood we will need. He buys the wood for the boardinghouse and can introduce me to his supplier.

All these new concerns. How I wanted to hear from Bishop Edington about the king's grant of a manor!—and about the solvency of that manor.

When I reached our house, Rebecca had just arrived a few minutes before and was taking some vegetables from her bag, preparing to make our evening meal. I offered my help, and she accepted, saying it had been a busy day at the tavern, and her feet were hurting. I took her in my arms and told her to sit, while I did the preparations and cooked our meal. She did, and I asked her what we would have with the vegetables she'd brought home.

She reminded me that we had packed the last bit of the beef roast in some salt and put it into a crock into the pit in the floor to stay cool. I brought it out and cut away a bit that looked to have mold on it; then put the rest into a cook-pot, along with some water, pieces of carrots, leeks, and an onion. I threw in some more salt and hung the pot over the fire-pit. This was traditionally considered woman's work, but times were changing, and we wanted to be part of the spring of new freedoms in learning and among the people.

While our meal cooked, I asked if she was feeling the baby move more each week. "Some days I do, and on others I don't. When I go two days without the feeling, I get worried that something might be wrong. Oh, Thomas! I so want this baby, so we will be a family! After my father died, my mother tried to fill his place, but the house seemed incomplete. I want our children to always have you and me to raise them. I pray that you and I can see them become adults with children of their own. She put her head on my chest and quietly wept. I was unsure what to say, and just held her close to me.

The cook-pot began steaming around the lid, and I eased it down at the table, so I could serve the meal. Her sadness seemed to have passed, and she asked if we might have a bit of wine. I poured her a small cup and one for myself, and we ate and talked until long after the food had been consumed.

When we retired for the night, I remained awake for some time after she had fallen into sleep, and I thought about who might be able to help her through her pregnancy, someone with experience in giving birth. My first thought was to ask the Widow if she could talk with Rebecca—at an appropriate time, once her pregnancy is confirmed—and offer her experience from birthing her own children. That idea gave me some comfort, and it allowed me to fall asleep.

The next morning I let her sleep a bit longer than usual and prepared for her some oatmeal with milk and berries that grew next to our house. I had it ready when she woke. Her sleep had been deep, and she was refreshed and pleased to have food already prepared. "Thank you for making me oatmeal—and for rubbing my feet last night! I should have less pain today at the tavern, as this day of the week usually has fewer customers for some reason. I won't need to run as much as I did yesterday.

"Perhaps, if you have the time, you could come to the tavern in the mid afternoon, when I can take a few minutes to have a bit of food, and we could talk."

"I will do that! I'll come at six hours past prime, at the bells of sext?"

"Yes, Thomas," and she kissed me on the nose at the implication of the oldest running joke in Christendom.

At the meeting house, I found Sir Arthur and Lord Morcant de Whatele, as well as Sir Ricard de Eynsham, whom I had not seen in several weeks. He had been gone to tend to matters at his manor west of town and had found that some men had raided one of his sheep pens. They'd torn down one wall of it and made off with twenty of his prize sheep. He stayed to oversee the rebuilding and to work with the sheriff. I could see in his face that he had yet to locate the lost sheep or the outlaws.

Sir Ricard had not been in Oxford for my election as coroner, and after his report, he rose to welcome me formally.

I appreciated his gesture and expressed my sorrow in the loss of his sheep. He told me that the sheriff had two of his deputies visiting all the farms and manors within ten miles of his, working on the thought that the thieves wouldn't want to travel very far for fear of being seen. There were several places left to be visited. I wished him good luck in locating the sheep.

This exchange had me thinking of the letter from our friend the lord treasurer about rounding up the major traitors running the double-leopards escapade to discredit the king and make a fortune while they were at it. But the humble image of the theft of sheep reminded me that the case was not entirely solved on the ground. What was a lord without his underlings?

I turned once more to look over the report we had prepared— with our credibility and possibly our lives so recently in the balance, line by line. Bishop Edington's letter, I now wondered, might imply that I should pick up where the investigators had left off, if indeed they had. Was he indirectly asking for more help? In fear of our lives, we may have reflexively rushed for help from higher-ups.

I was making notes to clarify my thoughts, when I looked up to find Houkyn standing by.

"Sir! said I—"

"You can dispense with the formalities, Coroner!" He cut me off with a smile.

"Sir Arthur," I insisted, "we have yet to solve the murder of the unknown man in Oxford, the body where you found the coins. The king's investigators have only caught the men at the top."

"So I heard from his lordship! What thoughts have you on

the subject, Coroner Thomas?" And he gave me a rarely seen grin.

De Whatele sidled up to see what we were about.

"Gentlemen," I continued, "we have a man dead on the ground. We have a bag of gold on the ground nearby. Strange. Did the perpetrator of the crime know there was gold on the ground? Not likely, as it still lay there to be found. He would have searched until he found it or returned for it before long. I think it is clear that the crime was committed for other reasons, for money, perhaps, but not for the coins on the ground. He knew nothing of them. That is significant, somehow." I paused for effect.

"Continue," said Houkyn.

"Now take the victim's point of view. If he was in possession of the coins and saw an attack coming, he might toss them aside. He would claim he had nothing on him. Or he might have lost the satchel in the grass and was searching for it when he was murdered. But—and here is the main question I would like answered—where did he get the coins?"

"Who knew such coinage existed?" Houkyn rejoined.

"Quite."

"So there appears to be at least a third party at the king's Reading mint."

"The dead man was not a lord, shall we say."

"No, he was, from his attire, by the laws of sumptuary, a commoner, an accountant, perchance? Someone who might have found discrepancies in the accounts."

"A case of blackmail?" I ventured.

"If he were one of the inner circle, he would be unlikely to be allowed to be out in the day with a stray satchel of double leopards! No, these were being shipped out of the country with special care."

"If their lordships sent one of their henchmen to silence this man, our dead blackmailer was a fool, not a professional in his trade, it would seem. That's my tuppence," offered de Whatele.

"And they would never tell the hired killer that there were

gold double leopards involved, to be sure," said I. "So no one looked for the coins, until our coroner's methodical craft discovered them hidden in the grass." I couldn't help thinking of the terror inflicted on us by the lurking Kenric Crouse, who had reportedly left town—to return to his master's manor.

"Thomas, though you are no longer our clerk, would you care to add these points to the report? Meanwhile we must find some corroboration, or we may never hear the end of such murders. We must know if there is an organized ring in league with lords of manors or who proffer their services to the same."

"You might solve more than one death, by the by," commented de Whatele, as he returned to his work.

The bells of sext called from their tower. A courier had showed up at the meeting house, with another letter from Bishop Edington. I opened it and repaired to the Hawk and Hare.

Alfred was there, and I joined him at one of the tables. Rebecca came round and, without entirely dropping her working manner, greeted me with a quick kiss. By coincidence, Alfred was curious to know if I had received any response from Treasurer of the Realm Edington. At Alfred's suggestion, I had written to request tax payments made for the three manors that the bishop had made available on behalf of the king.

"Yes, he has responded." I pulled out the letter. "Today!—"

"Wait!" said Rebecca, "I have a moment for a bite to eat, so I'll briefly join you for this news. Ale, Thomas?"

"And another for me, please," said Alfred.

She returned, and I reported on the letter, tucked away again, so as not to draw attention to its craftsmanship. "One of the three manors has paid very little in taxes in the recent annual filings, but the other two have afforded in excess of one hundred pounds each, assuming no one cheats the king."

"Quite so," intoned Alfred.

"I will visit the latter two manors to see them for myself, and evaluate which would be a better choice. As you know, Alfred, Rebecca and I need to have a more reliable source of funds,

now that I am a coroner, a position for which I will receive no
compensation. Fortunately, Bishop Edington has included in his
response the name of a landowner whom he knows, one John
Spencer, whom I met on the day of my election as coroner.

"Bishop Edington recommends I ask Spencer to visit the two
promising manors with me and advise on which would be the
better one to accept. Spencer, who lives in Oxford, has owned
an estate inherited from his grandmother, near Faringdon, for
nearly two decades, and with the assistance of a steward who
lives at the manor, he has made it very productive."

"Do ask Sir John if I might ride with you, please."

I did not mention that the name John Spencer rang in my
memory of the visit to the king's mint.

XIII

BETWIXT DOUBLE LEOPARDS

☙ ❧

As Alfred and I rode south towards Abingdon that
Saturday morning, I reviewed my list of questions for
Sir John Spencer, and Alfred offered some of his own. What
I wanted to learn were the characteristics of a productive
manor, how to find ways to improve a manor's profitability, and
especially the methods by which Sir John had brought his most
important workers to accept the new wage-based approach to
operating the manor. And how to find a steward who recognized
the benefits of a wage-based system.

Once Alfred and I had finished the review, we had the
opportunity to look about us at the land along the road and the
streams which flowed thereby. That got me thinking. Land is of
little value if there is insufficient water or lack of water during
the key times of the growing season. The better the stream,
the greener was the land through which it flowed. I added this
thought, which suddenly seemed strangely obvious, to my list.

The ride to Abingdon took about an hour and a half and
was enjoyable both for the company and the pleasure of being
out in such weather. As we neared the church in the center of
the village of Abingdon, the place where we were to meet, we

caught a scent and soon saw the source—the side of the church was covered with roses, and there was a buzzing of bees as they gathered the nectar that would soon be collected by the parson as honey, then perhaps also mead. Seated on his horse breathing in the fragrance, was Sir John Spencer, enjoying the late summer.

"Greetings, Sir John! I am pleased to see you again, and grateful to have the benefit of your experiences and learning gained from taking on your manor at Faringdon."

"I arrived but moments ago and was enjoying the lovely fragrance of the roses. I wish the roses which my wife has planted around our home were as fragrant as these. How was your journey?"

After introducing Alfred, I went straight to the question of water, and that got our guide started. "You have it exactly right. Our manor in Faringdon has a river on one border and two small but deep streams that pass clear through the property and flow in every month but in the depths of winter. Without these waters, our crops would grow much less, and the prices we get for those crops would be lower. Fortunately, we have yet to experience a drought, but we are digging a holding pond that we can fill from the river each spring by digging a trench that will allow water from the river to flow to the holding pond only when the river is at its highest level. The pond will provide water for our sheep and cows, who in turn will produce milk for making cheese that we sell. So your comment about the importance of adequate water supplies is quite correct, and we will look at the various ways to get water to the crops and livestock you raise on your renewed manor."

As the morning was more than half over, we set out to inspect one possibility of the king's treasurer's offerings.

Sir John, we discovered, after more than a decade operating his Faringdon manor in the traditional lord-and-villein arrangement, had made a major change a few years earlier. Recognizing that some few of his most important workers had approached him about being rid of their old traditional obligations to the lord of the manor, he came to the realization that workers were more likely to work and see their interests more closely connected to the estate, if they received some share of the wealth they helped create, in the form of wages. Sir John decided to try out this new but ancient philosophy with his eight most important workers, including his oxen driver, grain-mill operator, sheep shearer, and four lead plowmen.

He gathered them around the dining table at the manor house, quite unheard of, and told them he was willing to share with them a portion of the income the manor derived from their labor, and in return he asked that they begin seeing themselves as part of the management of the manor with responsibilities for overseeing the work done by those under their supervision.

Each one who agreed to this model of manorial management would receive a monthly cash payment that reflected the value of both their labor and of their oversight of those they supervised. He also promised them an additional payment following the autumn harvest or spring sheep shearing that would be a share of the manor's profits, after the manorial expenses were taken out. He did insist that none of them would, for the nonce, speak of his proposal with anyone outside this group of eight, and he asked that they meet again in one week to declare to him and the others in the group whether they would agree to this proposal.

When they met a week later, having recovered from their astonishment, each of the eight agreed to Sir John's proposal and pledged to him and their fellow workers to follow his plan for a year. If all were satisfied following the first year, they would agree to follow the plan one more year. After three years working under the plan, Sir John might expand the plan to include every worker, with the initial eight members working with him to set the wages for each job.

Ultimately, Sir John cancelled the status of villein and paid every worker the wages established for their jobs. The manor had become the most profitable in Oxfordshire, and the workers have used their wages to buy land from the estate to grow their own crops, send their oldest sons to learn to read and write, and to improve their homes.

Alfred and I were impressed with the experiment, to say the least, on ethical grounds, as well as profitability.

As we rode, Sir John asked how it came to be that King Edward III was giving me the choice of three Oxfordshire manors. At a leisurely pace to match the day, I told the story, answering questions that seemed to gain urgency. Finally I asked him directly if there was something I should know. But we had arrived at the manor, and the steward came forth to greet us.

Joseph Cotes had been the steward for the previous owner, who'd lost the estate because he had become involved with a scheme to ship wool to Italy, while bypassing the required tariff payments. Cotes had not been involved and was asked to remain until a new owner took possession. We met with him at the manor house and asked that he tell us about operations and productivity.

He duly went through the results for each of his four years' experience in charge. From the records, the manor had taken in more revenue from its operations in each year than the costs of producing the wheat, oats, sheep's wool, and incidental products, including cider, butter, milk and ale. It was a very helpful review of finances. I resolved to ask Sir John for his thoughts once we had left the house. So far he had been quiet, apart from a few pertinent questions and comments.

This property reminded me of my childhood and growing up on my father's estate. I decided to write to him for his thoughts before making of my final decision.

Coates invited us to feel free to inspect the property at our leisure.

I thanked him and we walked about the house, Sir John quietly noting the quality of its construction, the number of rooms on the three floors, the presence of glass in most of the windows, and a well appointed kitchen building adjacent—but just far enough removed so that a fire in the kitchen was unlikely to spread to the house. He pointed out that some of the floors needed restoration, as did a small section of the roof. On the whole, he considered the manor house worth the needed work.

Next we examined the barns, some of which were used to shelter horses, oxen, and the herd of milch cows, while others provided storage for the feed, as well as rooms for the workers who cared for the animals. Sir John was pleased with what he saw and noted minor repairs needed.

From the barns, we moved on to the houses occupied by the villeins and other workers who provided the labor and services that allowed the manor to earn the money it needed to be profitable. Here he noted that many of the houses were showing signs of deterioration and would need substantial work to make them properly livable and worthy of those whose work made the manor successful. He believed that those occupying those houses would be willing to do most of the repairs if the lord of the manor were to provide both materials and free time to allow the workers to make the repairs. I could feel the tension build again in his voice. He noted with restraint, almost under his breath, as though to himself, that he had done just what he was suggesting, and his workers had committed many hours to such improvements. "After the workers on my manor had repaired the houses in which they and their families lived, several told me that my willingness to assist them with the needed improvements to their homes showed them that what I was trying to do to make the manor more productive actually included helping them and their families to be better off."

When I replied off the cuff with a quip to the effect that I hardly imagined any would object, he drew in breath sharply as though my reaction was misplaced. But he said no more.

Next, we went out to the fields where the livestock and crops were grown and raised. The wheat and oats were approaching the point of being harvested, and Sir John commented favorably on the quality and quantity of both. He used his boot to dig into the soil in the wheat field and picked up a handful. "See how rich this soil is! It is almost black in color, an indication of significant amounts of material residue from the previous year's crop, and that makes the soil richer and more productive. By returning those residues back into the soil, the manor will continually improve the productivity of the land. This bodes well for you, should you select this estate. You would begin your ownership knowing the fields in which you plant your crops will provide you a good harvest." Then he added, "You will need to feel secure, of course."

I stood quietly waiting for him to be more forthcoming, with Alfred next to me about to boil over with the mounting tension of what should have been a routine inspection. Standing there in the open field, Spencer took us into his confidence. "You may as well know that I live daily with threats. Our Lord Bishop Edington is quite aware that I am regarded as an innovator. In some circles, the word 'radical' would be more to the point—a threat to the social order, to the divine order of things, even."

"What threats?" I reflexively replied, being coroner.

"Many and various, to my family, as well . . ." he tapered off and looked over the field to collect his emotions.

Here I was struck down in the midst of a dream of raising a family in pastoral contentment, while helping to better the world with reasonable justice. I looked at Alfred, who was quite pale and stood awkwardly now, digging the rich soil with his own boot. He kicked a clod in anger but remained silent.

"So," I concluded with abruptness, "we have much more to discuss than I thought. Our lord bishop, it would appear, has more in mind, as well. He knew this gift came with a price and is no doubt hoping I will—we will—help by solving the crime on the ground, so to speak."

Alfred looked me in the eye. "Making it personal."

"Indeed," said Sir John. "Work to be done."

* * *

On Saturday I was to meet Sir John to visit the second manor I was considering, this one located by the confluence of the Rivers Thame and Thames, about ten miles in a south-

southeasterly direction from Oxford, near Dorchester. It was available to me because its previous lord had died recently and left no heir to take over—causing the crown to repossess it.

At the designated time, we met at Oxford's south gate. Sir John had stayed at his Oxford home to spend time with his wife, Elizabeth, and their four children; the family never stayed long in the same residence, but moved more or less at random between town and their manor houses, with spontaneous sojourns and longer visits with friends and other family.

Sir John was somewhat unfamiliar with the area and seemed most interested in learning about what crops were raised thereabouts and if sheep had become a significant source of revenue.

The previous week he had told me about raising sheep and shearing their wool for sale to the wool merchants from the Italian states like Florence and to those trading centers along the European coast, in places like Bruges, Antwerp, and Amsterdam. These centers had begun to provide wool to local weavers and in return buy their woven products. Sir John said he considered devoting one of his manors solely to the raising of breeds of sheep that produced the best wool and selling the fleeces to the agents for the weavers' syndicate. I was quite interested in the idea and had some questions for him on the subject.

But as we rode towards nexus of the similar sounding rivers, the more pressing questions prevailed, rather about who might be getting fleeced—

Sir John laughed. Alfred had joined us again, and I heard him chuckle in spite of himself.

I was more than a bit in shock at a looming question as to whether I wanted to inspect the second manor or any manor henceforth. I kept it at bay, because of course I wanted manorial status and security—but even if I had to live as a slave master?— coroner of the law with ideals of reason and evidence? Not to mention being hunted by vengeful enemies who wanted my head on a gate post for a trophy. I was shaken to the very core of my idea of myself. I had not even confided in the love of my life—yet. I had to think and collect myself. Fortunately, at least one of us had experience in these risks and dilemmas. But Sir John was not in law enforcement, though he had deadly enemies in the courts—as well as at the king's court itself.

Who was right about him, therefore? Was he part of a criminal ring? Did he have a hand in the murder of "the accountant," as I had become accustomed to refer to the man who had presumably lost the satchel of double leopards? Had Bishop Edington handed me this knight of the realm to figure him out and bring him to justice? Why did the name "Spencer" appear on the list of suspects handed to Houkyn and me at the Redding mint? Was he a scapegoat? I burst out laughing.

The other two looked at me nervously. I looked at Sir John and saw a man who was trying to do something right in life. Did I have the strength to stand with him? I looked at Alfred, who had been so vital to my success from the start.

Sir John was glad to unburden himself meanwhile, and I tried to collect any clues amidst my worries and suspicions. My mind wandered. It was a good thing Alfred was there to keep the conversation moving along and to recall how it went.

We reached Thameside Manor by midmorning, and the steward, Jean Pepin, a Frenchman by birth, was waiting for us at the gates. After introductions, Alfred could not help but ask about the fate of the previous lord of the manor. "Died suddenly," came the terse reply.

"How?—I wonder," Alfred pursued while trying to appear casual, as though it was just part of regular enquiry about the estate.

"Unexpectedly—sire. Most unfortunate incident. Set upon by thieves, by all accounts. Came up the river."

"The River Thames?"

"Up from London, most likely. But I'm not a one to visit the city, much, can't say that I am."

He quickly mounted his horse and led us to the wheat fields. As we approached, it became clear that this year's crop was quite abundant. I asked Pepin what factors had helped produce such a robust crop.

"The presence of the rivers, sire. And regular rain during the growing season! The Thame feeds the Thames and both are fed by a number of streams and small rivers, providing good flow even during dry periods. We have built a canal to bring water to the crop fields during times when rainfall is less than what we need to produce good crops of wheat, oats, and a variety of vegetables that are in local demand. Fortunately we have not needed to draw water from the river very often this year, only two times."

A shiver coursed through me. Moral indecision summoned yet again the ghost of the rotting body of the thief at the crossroads. It brought nausea. I would discover that this manorial estate was even more favored than the other and by our great river of commerce. Here my wool could easily ship to world markets. By the same waterway, the crimes of the great city loomed, it seemed, like that doubt, now fed by tributaries.

The exceptional benefits of this beautiful property were met with even greater challenges. I was coming to terms with the reality that to find peace, I would be forever fighting crime. To own such a property, I would need to figure out the crime ring immediately at large on the land. In order to do so, I would have to figure out which side I was on, if sides even existed in these complex times. I idly wondered what the king was doing in France, anyway. Wasn't he fighting his own people who spoke the same language—French? I put the treasonous thought out of mind. Curse the double leopards!

XIV

NEWS

CȜ ȣɔ

I SPENT THE BETTER PART of dinner time reporting to Rebecca everything about my visit to Thameside Manor—the big house, the other buildings, the fields of ripening wheat and oats, the Rivers Thame and Thames flowing by the estate, and the channel from one of them to provide water when rain is insufficient. I paused and realized that in my distress I had not had the presence of mind to ask which river, and we had not inspected the canal.

I rallied and told her about the idea of developing a sheep herd and producing high-quality fleeces to sell to the buyers representing major users of wool in the weaving business. I expounded what Sir John Spencer had told me about the profits that are being earned by other English manors, which have recently developed sheep herds based on certain breeds whose fleeces were most desired by those weavers in Florence, Brussels, and Amsterdam. "Within a few years, Thameside Manor could be sharing in the ever-increasing demand for high quality fleeces—and the revenues those fleeces are bringing to other English sheep herders." All this, and no mention of wages, profit-sharing or death threats—not while she was with child.

I set aside any contemplation of when or how I would tell her, but I knew it would have to be done one day, for safety. And I set aside fears as to her reaction to what felt like a breach of trust between us, even though I was sparing her the distress of a reality that would shadow her life.

By the time she found out what she had got into with this man of property, it would be too late for her to participate in the decision, even though it would be obvious what she would choose with me—the manor. But would I look back one day after some tragedy and regret not having her decide with me, especially had she persuaded me to choose the other manor, away from the Thames.

Rebecca was of course excited and encouraged me to make a plan for developing a sheep herd soon after we take over our new estate. "What will we need to do to get started?" she asked.

I told her that Sir John would soon let me know the most desirable breeds to acquire to begin a herd. Then we should locate existing herds within ten miles of the manor to purchase sufficient sheep of that breed, and one or more rams. "Sir John told me that it would take two to three years to build the herd, before we would attract the fleece buyers' interest in what we can produce. But once the buyers become aware of our herd, they will be bidding against each other to purchase all of the fleeces we can produce each year."

Rebecca, being pragmatic, asked where we would obtain the money needed to start our herd. To that I reminded her that the manor is still growing crops and selling them to brokers, along with other products of the land. The income will enable us to begin buying the sheep and rams we will need, as well as allow you to stay home for the last months of your pregnancy, and still have money left.

That final thought led her to talk about the things we will need for the baby and our house. I agreed with some of what she wanted to purchase, but suggested we wait on other purchases, until we know how much the sale of the crops at Thameside would bring to us. "Keep in mind that some of those funds will be required for the new manor, for purchase of seeds, repair or purchase of equipment, and things about which we know nothing yet."

She admitted that she hadn't thought of the manor's needs, but hoped the sale of crops and manor-made goods would bring in substantial funds for all the needs.

The visit to the Thameside had left me more tired than I expected, almost as tired as Rebecca must have been every day now as she neared the birth of our baby, and we slept longer than normal on a Sunday. It was nigh on terce when we awoke and only then because someone was pounding on our door. I told her to stay in bed and went to see who was so insistent on rousing us.

I found a courier with a letter from my father. Such letters were not uncommon, but the urgency of the courier's knocking suggested some importance. He told me that the sender wanted him to deliver it directly into the hands of Thomas Votary, and I acknowledged that I was Thomas. I gave him a shilling for his delivery, and returned to our bed to share its contents.

I carefully opened the envelop to avoid ripping the letter, unfolded the pages within and began reading it to Rebecca. Father wasted no words getting to his purpose, and after reading the first few words out loud, I stopped speaking and scanned the following few sentences before tears filled my eyes.

Rebecca, seeing my pain, asked why I had stopped. All I could say was, "My brother is dead," and began to weep uncontrollably. She put her arms around my heaving shoulders and held me tightly for many minutes, until I was able to speak again. Through my tears, I told her that the letter said my brother, Augustus, had been killed while leading a charge against French soldiers.

Eventually, we finished reading the letter together in silence, such was our grief. Augustus had fallen during a skirmish in the battle with the French defenders at Caen in late July. The English army, led by our Plantagenet king against the French House of Valois, had succeeded in defeating the defenders of the city, allowing the English to march eastward and along the Seine River, chasing the Valois and seeking a strategic location, where they could engage them in a conclusive battle.

That was of course many years ago, as I write today. And this war between the houses of Plantagenet and Valois for the Kingdom of France never ends. My brother's life, for what? Both houses speak French, the language of the aristocracy, as do I, though I live and enjoy the English and its dialects of the everyday folk.

My father wrote that the word of Augustus's death had arrived just the previous day, in a hand-written note from King Edward, sent to Father by Bishop Branwardine. The bishop's dispatch regarding the Caen victory in July brought the first news of the Plantagenet army's early successes in the war to rule the largest kingdom in Europe. King Edward expressed his deep sorrow about Augustus's death in battle and told Father—who had, be it remembered, saved the king's life years before—that Augustus was an outstanding soldier and a true leader in warfare, and his loss would ever be mourned by His Majesty.

As touching and thoughtful as were the king's words, I could not accept that Augustus was gone. Though he and I had not seen each other in the past seven years, he was my hero, and his successes in the Plantagenet army made me very proud. Rebecca sought to comfort me, but there was no solace, just the raw pain of loss.

As the reality of Augustus's death sank in, I felt the need to see my father. It had been many months since I last saw him at our wedding, and I needed to share the grief with him. The next day I told my fellow coroners of my brother's death in battle and asked if I might take some days to travel to father's manor. They expressed their sadness and insisted that I go, and to take the time needed to grieve. I thanked them for their consideration and said I would leave in the morning.

I asked the Widow if she would check on Rebecca while I was gone and invite her for supper once or twice in my absence, to which she readily agreed. I would take her with me, but traveling on horseback might not be good for the baby. That was the advice the Widow offered, and I ever trusted her judgment.

The next morning I fixed Rebecca some hot oatmeal with honey, then left with my satchel for the stables to find Bayardine. Before we rode out the south gate of Oxford, I saw a street vendor selling strips of meat cooked on sticks and stopped to buy two of them to fill the void in my stomach. I had with me two apples, one for Bayardine and the other for me to eat along the road.

The weather that morning was just right for a ride. We trotted along the flat stretches of the main road going south and eased off to a walk when we came to any hills. A light breeze blew from the west, keeping the dust we stirred up and that of travelers we met coming north from blowing in our faces. We stopped at a spot where we could rest in the shade and she could eat her apple. I could hear the sound of a brook nearby, and I led her to a good drink before we returned to the road. There was no one hanging at the crossroads.

But as we rode on, I thought about how the death of Augustus was affecting me, and how much I would miss the talks we used to have, before he had to go with the king to France. He was six years my senior, but on Father's manor we were regular companions as children, until he went away for military training. Edward III was intent on building an army around a small group of his best soldiers, and Augustus was a member of that group, those destined to be officers leading the army into battle.

I wondered how he had died, and would have traded the victory at Caen for one more day with Augustus, and I wept many tears on the road. I thought of how word of his death must have hit my father, the cruel blow to a proud man who had weathered so many battles beside the king, survived despite the several wounds incurred, only to learn that his son's first wound was his last. And I hated the French soldier whose sword took my brother from me and hoped he had died in that battle.

Then I recalled the truth of our feudal system and the codes of chivalry. I renewed my resolve to accept the gift of Thameside Manor, establish Spencer's new management methods, and pursue a philosophy of reason and evidence. I would show some courage, like my brother had, though of a different kind. I would try to become a civilizing influence, however small, among the grand warring families of Europe.

With such thoughts, my tears gave way to hope, and I looked forward to seeing Father, though I would take care with radical ideas in connection with Augustus's death. I considered that the French were no more foreign to me than the Scots, so I would stay clear of politics in the midst of such emotion.

I arrived at the stables in the late morning, gave my horse over to a groom to be brushed and watered, and walked to the house. I found him, alone, in his bedclothes, sitting in a chair and staring out the window. I went to him, put my arms about his broad shoulders, said "Father—" before my own tears made further words impossible for several long moments. The look on his face showed how deeply Augustus's death had broken this strong and resilient man.

I drew a chair next to him, took his hand in my own, and told him I had come to mourn with him our loss. He didn't move or respond to my presence but just stared off into the distance, as if another son might come across the field, and my father would join him in death. The sadness that enveloped him and the room in which he sat seemed likely to hold him for the rest of his days. And I wept for what was not one, but two deaths.

Overwhelmed, I had to leave the room. I went to find his housekeeper to ask how long Father had been like this. A motherly woman named Clara Carpenter, she had come to the manor to care for my mother in her last few months of life and stayed on to care for the household. She told me that it had taken about day before he slipped away. At first he took some food and ale, but by the second day he ate nothing, and drank only water. He went to bed the first night, but in the morning he moved to the chair where I found him, and since then leaving only when she took his hand and led him to the privy.

"Thomas, you must find a way to bring him back to the living world, lest he be lost to us forever. I am so afraid for what is going on in his head. Please try!"

"Clara, I will do everything I can to break him free from the grip of this tragedy. But I will need your help. We must find a way through his grief, together."

"I will do anything you feel will help bring him round."

Feeling that nothing could be done at this time, I suggested we go to the warmth of the kitchen rooms and by the great fire think about ways we might break through his pain and sense of loss. Were things happening about the manor that made him happy? I wondered aloud. Projects he was doing with Joseph Farmer, his steward. "Or a new type of grain he wants to grow at the manor, or . . . and I trailed off and looked away, for I recalled that my father had been toying with some of the new ideas. I did not know how serious he might have got and whether he knew of the counter-currents that were building, from manor to manor, from the courtrooms to the royal court. At least the king was busy elsewhere—but to what extent had he become involved, no doubt inadvertently, with his double leopards gone astray? My thoughts whirled with my sorrow.

And then it came to me. "The baby we are expecting in a few months! New life coming into our family and filling the void! Of course!

"Father knows that Rebecca and I are having our first child very soon, and if we can get him thinking of his first grandchild, the joy of new life may bring him back in order to see, hold and love our new baby. I can think of nothing more powerful to pull him out of his deep mourning."

"Oh, Thomas! What a wonderful idea! Before he heard of Augustus's death, he spoke often of having a grandchild and took great pleasure in telling us how he was looking forward to holding the baby in his arms. If anything can bring his mind back towards life, new life, the birth of your baby, his grandchild, will be it."

"Clara, you know my father's moods better than I. What time of day would be the best for me to speak about our soon-to-be-born baby? I want my words to have the most beneficial effect on him."

"Before he heard about Augustus's death, his best time of day was in the early afternoon. By then he had oft dealt with the day's issues of the estate and was thinking about what he could do to make improvements. I suggest that you speak to him at that time of day."

"I thank you, Clara!"

I began considering how to achieve the best result from my words to Father. It seemed to me that I needed to start from the reality of my brother's death and then remind him of the new life that will soon enter our family. I considered telling him that if our baby is a boy, that we will name it after Augustus. But I worried that doing so might make him feel like we are pushing Augustus into the background. If I took this approach, I would need to emphasize that naming the baby after him was to honor and remember Augustus.

My alternative would be to simply remind him of the child that soon would become part of his family, and how important a grandfather will be in our baby's life. The more I thought about the options, the more I leaned towards the latter approach. It seemed the best way to draw him, again, towards life.

In the early afternoon I sought him out as he sat in his chair, and drew up a chair next to his. "Father, I want to tell you about Rebecca's and my hopes and plans for our first baby—and your first grandchild. The babe will be born within the next two months, and we want to have you visit us soon after the birth. Rebecca asked me to tell you what we have done to prepare for this blessed event. We have moved to a house we are renting in Oxford and are obtaining such things as a cradle, where the baby will sleep next to our bed, along with blankets, warm fabric to wrap about the child during the day, and such other items as will make it easier to provide care and feeding. We will stay at the house this winter, while I work with Sir John Spencer, Lord of an Oxfordshire manor, who has found new ways to increase the profitability of his estate, while building a loyal group of workers, who will share a portion of the manor's earnings after expenses are paid.

"He and I, along with a friend, Alfred Rowley, visited two manors of the three offered to me by King Edward. Based on our evaluation of the assets and shortcomings of each, I have chosen the one near Dorchester, where the two rivers, Thame and Thames, come together, as you know. Thameside offers the greatest potential to produce revenues well in excess of its expenses.

"When the weather warms in the spring, I will divide my time between Oxford and my duties as one of its coroners and Thameside, where I will work with the steward, Jean Pepin to develop improvements. With the advice of Sir John Spencer, we will add sheep as a new source of income for the near future.

"Sir John considers Thameside an outstanding choice for Rebecca and me, one that offers protection against drought and good access to fleece buyers, once our flock is developed.

"Thameside is of course not far from here and from Oxford. We look forward to regular visits from you at both our homes— in Oxford and at the manor. Our baby will benefit greatly from knowing and loving his grandfather, and Rebecca will also, as her father died when she was young, and she never knew him."

I was not expecting a response from my father on anything I had said but hoped that what he heard from me might give him reason to want to live on and see his grandchild grow up. I was surprised when he asked what name our baby would have, and I took a deep breath before responding.

"We have considered names for a daughter or a son, and Rebecca has proposed that if it is a girl, we name her after my late mother, Virginia. And if it is a boy, to name it after her late father, John. What do you think of those choices?

He said nothing for a few moments, then spoke. "I approve

both names, but ask that if it is a boy, that his second name be Augustus!"

I was surprised but pleased with his request and told him that I had no doubt that Rebecca would happily agree to it. Leaning over, I put my arms about his shoulders and held him close for some time, telling him that I had feared that I would never hear him speak again. Then we sat, side by side, quietly enjoying his turn back to life and to family.

"One more thing, Thomas." He looked in my eyes. "Take care!" And he gripped my arm painfully. "Take care, Thomas—with Spencer!" And he let go and slumped back into his chair.

He now had a weary but present aspect, staring into the flames that warmed and lit the shadows of his sitting room. "I accept that your marriage to Rebecca, the daughter of a villein, is the future, no doubt. Just assure me, Thomas, as it be so, let there be one—I cannot lose another!"

To my surprise, I heaved a sigh of relief.

XV

GATHERING OF WAYS

౪ ౸

I ARRIVED IN OXFORD IN the mid afternoon, brought Bayardine to the livery stable, and walked to the Hawk and Hare to see Rebecca, have an ale while waiting for her to finish her day's work. It had been a slow day at the tavern, and she was able to take two breaks while I was there, both times coming to sit at my table and rest her feet. In those brief respites I was able bring her up to date about my father, but said nothing about his warning in connection with Sir John Spencer. I had asked Father also to say nothing of this until I had a chance, after the baby was born, and of course he agreed to leave it to me.

"You have done a wonderful thing in bringing your father back from the depths of his sorrow and despair. I hope he will visit us after our baby is born, in time to see the child christened. We will certainly give our baby a second name that honors your father and Augustus."

A week before she went into labor and delivered our baby, we agreed that if the baby was a girl, her name would be Maria Leorica Augusta Votary. A son was born and a month later christened Robert Leoric Augustus Votary. Robert was a healthy, full-voiced addition to our family and was doted upon by our growing circle of friends and colleagues. He never lacked for attention or companionship from the several young women who had become friends with us in the past year. While Rebecca stayed at home to care for him, she often had company. She was glad to have others around, as Robert slept for long stretches during the day, and the conversations helped pass the time. If she or Robert had a need, there was someone available to assist by running an errand or watching the baby while Rebecca went outside to walk about and stretch her legs.

The conversations with her several companions helped her know more about raising Robert, filling the void she felt because her mother was not there to help and guide her in bringing up our son. More than once she told me of what she had learned that day from one of her friends who has raised a child. It was clear that she was missing her mother, but her friends were helping to fill the void.

The arrangements for the christening were finalized a week before the event, and the Widow had let me know that Clara, if she came with my father, would have a room at a boardinghouse just around the corner from her own where Father would stay.

With the christening under control, I went to the coroners' meeting room to see if I was needed on any matter. To my great surprise and pleasure, I found Houkyn in conversation with John, the villein who had helped us uncover aspects of the theft of the double leopards. They halted their conversation when I walked in, and John rose to greet me warmly.

"How are you, John? And your family? I have thought about you many times, and hoped we would see you again." I took a seat at the table and John sat back down. "We owe you a great deal—not least freedom for you, your wife and young child. We know Lord de Glissaude is in the king's gaol in London, awaiting trial for treason. Are you still living at Longate?"

I confess that I felt a pang of guilt. Here I had been riding high, choosing between two manors, without having attended to our promise to a man enslaved, who had helped me to my new prospects. As we had not gone to him, he had now come to us.

But he replied graciously. "We're still there at Longate, sire, reunited as we are, and so times is better than when last I saw you. But I came to Oxford to seek out Sir Arthur and your good self, hoping that you can help me get our freedom. So I can seek work, sire, where I can use my skills to make a better life for myself and my family."

I felt suddenly disoriented by this simple statement and request.

Houkyn spoke up. He looked straight at me and slowly said that he and John had been discussing what might be done to assist him. "I suggested that we might appeal to Lord Bishop Edington to grant John his freedom, Thomas. We can write to His Excellency, explaining the situation, and our commitment to John—that we would help him be rid of any legal obligations to whomever became the owner of Longate Manor, freedom for the family."

I recalled my decision to be proactive in bringing about change, facing the risks, fighting crime, not running away. "Excellent," Sir Arthur! And if you, John, are interested in being the assistant steward at my manor on the Thames, I will pay you well, be pleased to have your services, and provide an apartment where you and your family can live.

"Thameside is the manor. It's just by Dorchester. The River Thame, a tributary of the Thames, you know, runs nearby as well. I will admit freely, you played a part in obtaining such a property for me!"

I felt better. I pulled out a pad of paper and forthwith began to write an addendum to the carefully crafted document we had sent Bishop Eddington. The story of John's assistance to us in discovering the scheme concocted by the Reading mint's manager and Lord de Glissaude, whereby they stole many of the golden double leopards, upon which the king himself relied for his honor and prospects in the European world—I would summarize, repeating the relevant sections of the document.

As I wrote in silence, the world seemed turned upside down, and I had be sure not to mix up the words "king" and "villein," which seemed to have resonance in common. Then I looked up from the table. Did I even know the full story? Houkyn and John were chatting like old friends with memories in common. Houkyn looked over at me and declared, "Thomas, surely you can complete that later!"

"Indeed, but I thought to have it all here for John to confirm I had left nothing out. Now I realize I may have left out some questions. For example, John, did Bishop Edington's men ever question you, and if so to what extent, I wonder."

I saw John blanch, and I quickly restated my question. "Surely they did not threaten you!"

"No, sire, no threats were made, but they did ask me a few things; not as much as they might have, mind you."

"And I can imagine that you did not wish to interfere anymore than was required of you."

"Yes to that! Tongues are withdrawn where they be not withheld, betimes—"

"And you have kept your ear to the ground, I dare say?"

"You know I have at that, sire!"

Houkyn picked up on my line of questioning, "So you gave evidence enough for the higher-up to be taken, but closer to home, shall we say, things are as they were?"

"As they were, sire, with the exception that my wife and child were rescued—"

"It seems, Thomas, that Edington has bigger fish to fry, and we local coroners are left to do the rest, whatever that may be."

I put down my pen. "Left to connect Coroner de Adynton giving away to his co-conspirators the fact of our journey with the double leopards to Reading—with the murder of a local man."

I turned to John and asked plainly, "How much do you know of a local clique, a crime ring, my good man?"

"Many know what they dare not say—"

"So your wife and child were insurance against your silence?"

"Good insurance."

"Why did they choose you, John, of all good folk, to steal the gold coins from us at the inn?"

"Because, I know a thing or two, as you might want to say, or might want me to say. They had to send someone who could be a guilty party, a scapegoat. I was not in the ring, but I keep my eyes and ears open, and they know it. It was a way to take care of that as well, if you take my meaning, sire. They wouldn't bring in a complete outsider for a job like that, knowing about gold coins and all that. Word might just get round outside the rings!"

"Rings?" asked Houkyn.

"It's complicated, well for the likes of me, anyways."

"I think you're less than too clever by half, my friend," Houkyn replied with a warm smile of encouragement. "Well Thomas, either we have an easier time of it—solving crimes in the area by hanging it on these rings—or we have more work cut out for us than we ever imagined. It's one thing chasing down random crimes, quite another an organization—or two or three."

"No more than that, sire, surely," said John. And we waited for something more.

"Well, o' course, it's the divisions between classes of folk, mainly. There are plainly many levels in law, who can wear what and whatnot, but in the criminal world some divisions get overlooked for practical purposes, so that makes the thing simpler, you might say. But the clique that has the most weight owns the land, to be sure. For example, Mr. Votary, does the name Carouse say anything to ye?"

I said nothing, while I could see he watched the sweat break out in my face.

"Well, you see, the man is just nobody, really," he continued with ease. "An example of a subservient organization, but a ring in itself, you might say. Because they are organized, they move from one place to another and talk—and talk will travel. I have always had big ears, can't be helped."

Both coroners couldn't help seriously sizing up his ears, and we all laughed at once, albeit nervously.

"Carouse, he is one of the slave ring, sex slaves, bounty hunters for runaway villeins, of course," John added breezily. "As well as being a job hunter. Was going to look him up myself, if I ever got free. Beggars can't be choosers—and we know what happens to a sturdy beggar before the law! Has a bit cut off—" He glanced at the floor, feeling he had overstepped.

"John," I asked earnestly, "was the murdered man the accountant? The one who was found with the double leopards nearby him? We think he might have been blackmailing their lordships, without knowing who he was challenging, and without experience in the craft, I might add."

"You got that right, poor sod!" I mean him, of course. What I mean is—"

"John, we know what you mean, and we vouch for your honesty in being forthcoming. May you be as free as a freeborn Englishman!"

"I think we have much to discuss, the three of us," concluded Houkyn. "Down the pub for the rest, shall we? Find a corner to talk in confidence over a pint, anyone? A step in the right direction!"

"I'm sure we can find a coroner, at any rate!—beggin' your pardon," said John with a silly grin.

It was gladly approved. The written report could wait, until I had figured out how much to reveal and to whom.

I trusted Bishop Edington to act affirmatively on behalf of John and his family but believed that it would take some time to go through the hands of more than one official before a document could be prepared and issued granting manumission to all three. I told John as much and that I was sure he and his family would be released from their manorial obligations.

Over our brews, John regaled us with a blow by blow description of de Glissaude's arrest at the manor, down to the look on his face and a description of the manacles.

Eventually I said, "John, I will be meeting with Sir John

Spencer in the near future to discuss how to change the relationship between the workers and myself, along the lines of what Spencer has been able to accomplish. I would like you to join us for that conversation, as I believe your life experiences and ability to see the interests of both sides will make that discussion more productive. As assistant steward at the new manor, your key role in the first year will be to build trust with the workers regarding changes to manor operations that will give them a share in the profits—" I stopped short to study his expression.

"Mr. Votary, it is a wonderful and revolutionary idea, and I will defend it with my life, you can depend on it, sire!"

* * *

Rebecca was nursing Robert when I got home, and I sat nearby to observe how she managed him. As he nursed, he had his eyes closed and a most blissful look on his face, which was reflected in Rebecca's. She looked up briefly to smile at me, then closed her eyes while humming for Robert. This union of mother and son during nursing is ever with me.

When Robert finished nursing and slept, she carefully placed him in the cradle and came to welcome me home with a kiss. I told her how beautiful she looked while nursing him, and she smiled. "How was your day, Thomas? You were gone longer than usual. Was there something going on that required the involvement of the coroners?"

"There was, but it was something good. You have heard me speak of John, the young man sent to steal back the gold coins Houkyn and I carried with us when we went to Reading to investigate. He was at the meeting room when I arrived, and we had much to discuss. He told us about the last day of freedom for the Lord of Longate, how he was captured by the king's guards. The king's men had his manor house surrounded and caught him trying to slip away down a trail seldom used.

"John has been assisting the man sent by Bishop Edington to manage the Longate until such time as a new owner takes over;

John has learned much. That experience will prove useful, as I plan to hire him to be the assistant steward at Thameside."

"I find it a bit strange that you wish to employ the man who tried to steal the gold coins at the inn. I know you found him very helpful during the investigation—and I know he was acting under threat from his master. And we don't suspect him of murdering the young man—do we? But can you truly trust him?"

"Yes, I am quite certain that he can be trusted. And, given our Lord Bishop Edington's consideration of the important role John played in uncovering the conspiracy to steal more of the king's special gold coins, I expect that John with his wife and son will be emancipated. This will make them and their offspring free in perpetuity."

"I trust your judgment and truly hope that His Excellency will see that John and his family are freed from all previous obligations of the bondage and of the status of villein, as you can imagine."

I asked Rebecca if she would meet John sooner than later, as I believed he would win her over by his humility and his commitment to us, even his sense of humor.

* * *

In due course, a package and letter arrived from His Excellency, who said he was unable to get away from governmental duties and his recent appointment as Bishop of Winchester. But he sent along a gift for Robert Leoric Augustus Votary and a letter to be given to John of Longate Manor as soon as the latter arrived in Oxford.

I was so pleased to have my father with us, and we quickly arranged a dinner at which several of our friends joined us to meet him. Before dinner, Father took me aside and told me that he and Clara had discussed the idea of marriage to each other but wished to have my blessing. I was touched by their asking me and told him that I heartily agreed. I told him that when he was deep in mourning and nothing we tried was able to rouse him from his sadness, it was Clara who inspired the idea of bringing home to him the impending birth of baby Robert. I saw the tears well up in his eyes. I put my arm around his shoulder, and told him that nothing would make me happier than for him and Clara to wed.

As our guests arrived, I introduced each of them to my father, and told him a bit about each one. Soon he was deep in conversation with Alfred and Sir Arthur, wanting to know more about them and telling some stories of his time with King Edward during the war against the Scots—with whom, by the by, I had gained some increased sympathy, which I kept to myself as though they were French.

Clara had not met Rebecca before tonight, and they talked about many things, particularly about raising babies, and quickly they became close friends. This was more of a relief to me than I had expected. The underlying fact regarding my marriage to the daughter of a villein, though she was now free, was abiding and potentially more dangerous than I had known. Now with my family's greater support and with the hard-earned wisdom of John and more-than-a-bit-less naïve myself, I felt I could fight for the common good.

* * *

The christening turned out to be a celebration of more than one name. I had invited John and his wife Margaret and their child Antonia up to Oxford the day before to gather at our house, meet Rebecca, and open the envelop from Bishop Edington.

It was a letter of freedom for all three. There were tears and laughter, and we brought out an intimate pre-christening feast, thankful that it was graced with the good news on which we had planned. Perhaps we would have needed the sustenance all the more had the letter gone the other way. My father was so caught up in the emotion that after a glass of our best wine, he was saying political things I will not repeat. We joked that we had become our own little subversive folk ring.

Maurin Barrett was there, that trusted fellow, who had helped me take over from him as coroners' clerk. He had said he would not miss the christening for all the world, and the Widow Rowley had found space again for him to stay. A rather continuous celebration had already got momentum, and I was wondering how long the festivities might take hold with everyone in Oxford. I was prepared to stay the course!

After dinner, Maurin dropped into a wooden chair next to me and said, "Coroner Votary!"

"Yes Maurin?"

"Would you like me to solve the case of the murdered girl, Alice?"

"You know it remains unsolved—"

"Does it, now?"

"Let's have it, then. I am all ears with a full belly, and we have both had too much to drink, no doubt."

"Yes, you are right—not the proper occasion for such talk. Another time."

We sat in silence and sipped our claret.

"Well," I said finally. "Out with it, so we can continue with the celebrations."

"That man Hunter—"

"Ah yes, the nervous juror!"

"He shows up at the manor, on the sly rather. And Father wants to know what he is doing out and about with no apparent purpose or introduction. Word had got round that Hunter was in the neighborhood. Good name for one who is looking for skilled villeins, don't you think? I suppose one can't blame him, really—such meager prospects, what?"

I was fairly sure we were both thinking of John, his family, and Rebecca.

"Well, Hunter wasn't such a rum fellow after all. We brought him into the big house, gave him a glass of sherry, and settled in before the great fireplace for a chat. Father is a wily old sort. Not sure we can turn back all the changes happening on the estates, but sex slavery is always one to fight, that's for sure."

"So, Alice was being forced into slavery, rape! How?"

"They can be extremely persuasive. If the crime ring is in the business of finding freedom and skilled or wage-paying jobs, then it's easy enough to have the credibility to entice folk in hard circumstances into even worse—"

"So simple," was all I could say.

"She must have balked and got wise—threatened them to lay off her."

"And they just murdered her and moved on."

"Hunter was nervous with the knowledge and all the rest he knew. My ol' dad, he knows a thing or two, though. Set him at ease and got the story."

"Some of it anyways."

"Some."

I thought of all that John might be able to tell me in times to come. I resolved to listen carefully, as though our lives depended on it. And then to act, strategically, for years to come.

"John wants to name his family after Thameside," said I.

"It's good name, but for an ex-villein of the land, best to be with a river—John Thames."

He'd overheard us. "Here am I, sire! John Thames, at your service."

"Thomas, John; you will call me Thomas, whatever anyone might say."

He looked at me carefully and replied, "That might depend on who's listenin', Thomas!"

"Gentlemen," I replied, "I am learning that in setting out to solve a crime or two, I have been chasing the effects of deeper causes. The task may seem worse than I had thought, but I would have been chasing my tail without the likes o' John to call me out."

We laughed, but John objected to being a gentleman. "Though manners maketh man, Thomas, I grant ye that."

CB BD

Richard Davies

Photo Ramona du Houx

The author has always been an avid reader fascinated with medieval history. Drawn to the origins of democracy and the changes in society that led to the system that gives people rights, he focused on exploring the issue further and has written his first novel.

Richard Davies holds a BA and MA in history from the University of Maine and was awarded a Ford Foundation Fellowship, serving as staff historian for the Ford Foundation's interdisciplinary investigation into the environmental degradation of the Penobscot River in Maine.

While in graduate school, he was elected to the first of four terms in the Maine House of Representatives for the town of Orono.

From 1982 Davies served as legislative director for Governor Joseph Brennan. And from 1987, he worked for the Maine State Housing Authority, founded Public Policy Associates, Inc., and worked as a senior policy advisor for Governor John E. Baldacci.

He then became the state's public advocate, representing the interests of consumers of utility services in proceedings before the Maine Public Utilities Commission.

Davies was elected Kennebec County treasurer in 2013 and reelected in 2017.

"Dick has been a key public servant who progressed the quality of life for all the people of Maine throughout his career. He embodies the principles of democracy in all his actions." —Gov. John E. Baldacci